Scribe Publications
THE ETERNAL SON

CRISTOVÃO TEZZA, one of Brazil's foremost contemporary novelists, was born in 1952. He has published thirteen novels, including *O Filho Eterno* (*The Eternal Son*), which won every major literary prize in Brazil in 2008 and has been translated into seven languages. He was also the recipient of the Brazilian National Library Award in 1998 and the Brazilian Academy of Letters Award in 2004.

Additionally, he teaches Portuguese at the Federal University of Paraná, and has published textbooks and articles in a number of magazines and newspapers. He is presently working on a book of short stories. Tezza lives in Curitiba, in the south of Brazil.

ALISON ENTREKIN has translated a number of works by Brazilian and Portuguese authors into English, including *City of God* by Paulo Lins and *Budapest* by Chico Buarque, which was shortlisted for the 2005 *Independent* Foreign Fiction Prize in the UK. Originally from Australia, she now lives in Brazil.

For Ana

The
ETERNAL SON

Cristovão Tezza

Translated by Alison Entrekin

SCRIBE
Melbourne

Scribe Publications Pty Ltd
PO Box 523
Carlton North, Victoria, Australia 3054
Email: info@scribepub.com.au

First published in Portuguese as *O Filho Eterno*
in Brazil by Editora Record 2007

Published in Australia and New Zealand by Scribe 2010

This work was published with the support of the Brazilian
Ministry of Culture/National Library Foundation/General
Department of Books and Reading.

Obra publicada com o apoio do Ministério da Cultura
do Brasil/Fundação Biblioteca Nacional/Coordenadoria
Geral do Livro e da Leitura

 MINISTÉRIO DA CULTURA
Fundação BIBLIOTECA NACIONAL

Typeset in 12/17 pt Adobe Caslon Pro by the publishers
Printed and bound in Australia by Griffin Press
Only wood grown from sustainable regrowth forests is used in the
manufacture of paper found in this book.

National Library of Australia Cataloguing-in-Publication data

Tezza, Cristovão, 1952-

The Eternal Son

9781921372988 (pbk.)

869.342

www.scribepublications.com.au

We wish to tell the truth but fail to do so.
We describe something truthfully, but our description
is something other than the truth.
Thomas Bernhard

A son is like a mirror in which the father beholds himself,
and for the son the father too is like a mirror in which he beholds
himself in the time to come.
Søren Kierkegaard

'I think it's today,' she said. 'Now,' she added, her voice stronger, touching his arm because he was absent-minded.

Yes, he was absent-minded, possibly. Someone makeshift, perhaps; someone who, at the age of twenty-eight, still hadn't begun to live. Strictly speaking, except for an array of happy anxieties, he didn't have anything, nor was he anything yet, exactly. And this walking, talking bag of bones, full of aggressive, oft-times offensive cheer, saw himself before his pregnant wife almost as if he had only now understood the full extent of the fact: a baby.

'So today's the day,' he said, laughing expansively. 'Let's go!'

His wife, who had supported him in every sense for the last four years, was now supported by him while waiting for the lift, at midnight. She was pallid. Contractions. My water, she said, or something to that effect. He didn't think a thing — as far as newness went, tomorrow he'd be as new as his baby. In the meantime, he needed some make-believe. Before leaving, he'd remembered to slip a little cowboy-style flask of whisky into his other pocket. In the first were his cigarettes. A cartoon: a character chain-smokes in a waiting room until a nurse, a doctor, someone shows him a little bundle and says something funny, and we laugh. Yes, there's something funny about the wait. We role-play, the anxious father, the happy mother, the crying baby, the smiling doctor, the stranger who appears out of nowhere and congratulates us — the vertigo of a time now desperately speeding up, everything spinning quickly and inevitably around a baby, to only come to a halt some years later, sometimes never. The role came with a whole scenario, and in it one must appear to be happy. Proud, too. He'd deserve respect. There was a whole dictionary of things one should say about a birth.

In a way — now he was trying to start his yellow vee-dub (they didn't say anything, but they felt something good in the air), taking care not to scrape the mudguard on the pillar, as he'd already done twice — he was being born now as well, and he liked this more-or-less edifying image. Even though he was still elsewhere. This was a constant feeling, which is why he smoked so much, an inexhaustible machine demanding fuel. It was a whole terrain of ideas: standing in it, we have nothing, just the expectation of a vague, sketchy future. But I don't have anything yet either, he might have said, in a kind of metaphysical competition. No house, no job, no rest. Come to think of it, I do have a son — and, always joking, he imagined himself pot-bellied, severe, finally working on something solid, a perfect portrait of the family on the wall. No, his was a different sphere of life. He was predestined for literature — someone necessarily superior, an individual for whom the rules of the game were different. Nothing ostentatious: true superiority was discreet, tolerant, and smiling. He lived on the fringe, that was all. He didn't feel resentment because he wasn't mature enough yet for resentment — a force that can come along and aggressively put us in our place. Perhaps the origins of this counter-force (though he had no way of knowing, being too close to the present) lay in the fact that he'd never been able to make a living from his work. From his true work. This was a tension that almost always escaped in laughter, the only release available to him.

At the maternity-ward counter the woman politely asked for a cheque, and things moved too quickly because someone was leading his wife away. Yes, yes, her water's broken, he heard, while doing the paperwork — once again he had a hard time filling in his profession, and almost said, 'The one with the profession is my wife. I ...' He still found time to say something — his wife, too — but in front of other people their affection became ceremony. It seemed that something bigger was taking place, a kind of theatre insinuated itself (we are too delicate for this matter of birth and need to disguise life's dangers) as if someone — and the image was absurd — was leading his wife to her death, and it was completely normal. He once again felt his horror of hospitals, of public buildings, of solemn institutions, of columns, foyers, reception desks, domes, queues, of their granitic stupidity — and the grammar of bureaucracy was repeated here too, in the small, private space of the maternity ward. Later, he found himself in a room gazing at his wife on a stretcher. Pallid, she smiled at him and they touched hands timidly, almost as if they were breaking the rules. The sheet was blue. There was a sterility about everything, a brutal absence of objects, footsteps echoed as if in a church, and again the falseness bothered him. There was a primary error somewhere, and he couldn't work out where; but he quickly let the thought go. The seconds slid past.

Someone said something that he didn't hear, and he lost all track of the hours as he waited. 'What time is it?' Late. Now he was alone in a corridor next to an empty ramp facing two swinging doors with round windows that he peeked through from time to time, but saw nothing. He didn't have a single thought but, if he had, it might have been: I am as I have always been — alone. Then, lighting a cigarette, happy: and that's good. He took the whisky out of his pocket and had a sip, acting out his little pantomime. For now, things were good. He didn't think about his baby — he thought about himself, and that included the totality of his life, wife, child, literature, future. He knew he'd never written anything really good. Just piles of bad poetry, from the age of thirteen until last month: 'The Son of Spring'. Poetry dragged him mercilessly into kitsch, pulling him by the hair, but something needed to be said about what was going on, though he didn't know exactly what was going on. He had a vague feeling that things were going to work out fine because he wanted them to, and people on the fringe, like himself, took risks — either that or be slotted into the sub-life of the system, that load of crap, he almost declaimed, taking another sip of whisky and lighting another cigarette.

At twenty-eight he was still doing a degree in Language and Literature, which he loathed, he drank a lot, laughed long and inconveniently, read chaotically, and had a drawer brimming with texts. An old hook still held him to the nostalgia of an actors' community, which he visited once a year because of a prolonged dependence on his childhood guru, struggling endlessly and hopelessly to adjust today's clock to the phantasmagoria of a time long gone. Still clinging to the 1970s, filled with the pride of the periphery of the periphery, he used his intuition to sniff out a solution. Being reborn is hard, he'd say some years later, colder. Meanwhile, he tutored a few pupils in essay writing, and painstakingly proofed master's theses and dissertations on any subject. Grammar was an abstraction that allowed for everything. He'd quit being a watchmaker — or, rather, the profession, a medieval dinosaur, had quit him. If only he'd had a gift for business, behind a shop counter. But, no, he'd chosen to fix watches, because of a childlike fascination for mechanisms and the useless delicacy of manual work.

Nevertheless, he considered himself an optimist. He smiled, seeing himself from above, as he had in his imagined cartoon, now a real person. Alone in the corridor, he took another sip of whisky and started to feel the euphoria of the father being born. Things were fitting together. The perfect portrait on the wall. He laughed at the paradox, almost as if the simple fact of having a child entailed his definitive induction into the system, which wasn't necessarily bad, as long as one was 'whole', 'authentic', 'true'. He still liked these lofty-sounding words coming from his own mouth, the myth of the powers of natural purity versus the dragons of artifice. He was already starting to have doubts about these rhetorical absolutes, but he lacked the courage to part with them — the truth be told, he had never completely freed himself of this folklore, which meant he had to stay on his toes, alert, his whole life, so as not to be devoured by the violent and fathomless power of the trite and impersonal. He needed 'truth' to emerge from rhetoric and become a permanent restlessness, a brief utopia, a sparkle in his eyes.

Like now, and he took another sip of whisky, almost entering the terrain of euphoria. He wanted to create a sense of ritual for that moment, a ritual that was all his own. Like the director of a play walking an actor through a scene: You sit down like this, then you go over there and smile. Look how you take out a cigarette, sitting alone on this blue bench, while you wait for your baby. You cross your legs. You think about how you didn't want to watch the birth. Fathers watching their children being born is 'in' now, an almost religious participation. Everything seems to be becoming religion. But you didn't want to, he imagined himself saying. It's just that my world is mental, he might have said if he'd been older. A child is the idea of a child; a wife is the idea of a wife. Sometimes things coincide with our ideas of them; sometimes they don't. They almost always don't, but time goes on and we occupy ourselves with new things, which fit into new families of ideas. He hadn't even wanted to know if it was a boy or a girl: the heavy shadow of the echogram, that primitive phantom projected on a small screen, moving in the darkness and warmth, didn't translate into a gender, just a being. 'We'd rather not know,' they'd told the doctor. Everything seemed fine; that was what mattered.

There, finally, he felt as if time was standing still, suspended. In that well-lit silence, in which tiny, distant sounds (footsteps, a door closing, a low voice) took on the gravity of a brief echo, he thought about the change in his life and tried to imagine a routine, so that things wouldn't change too much. He had more than enough energy to spend days and days sleeping poorly, drinking beer in the intervals, smoking a lot, laughing and telling stories, while his wife recovered. Now he was going to be a father, which always dignified one's biography. He'd be an excellent father, he was sure: he'd make his child the arena for his view of the world. He already had a whole explanation of the universe ready for him. He remembered a few verses of 'The Son of Spring'. His lecturer friend was going to publish it in the university literary magazine. Yes, the lines are beautiful, he thought. Poets were good with advice. Do this, be like that, breathe this air, look at the world — metaphors, one by one, evoked human goodness. A Kipling of the province, he felt impregnated with humanism. My child will be the ultimate proof of my qualities, he almost said out loud, in the silence of that last corridor, a few minutes before his new life began. It was as if the communal religious spirit secretly flourishing at the heart of the country, the whole dream of natural utopias with its soft irrationalism and ethereal transcendence, the celestial peace of God's lambs now revived without frontiers, rituals, or textbooks (everything goes, oh Lord!), had also found refuge in the fringe poet, perhaps in him above all. The irrational undertaking of utopias: long hair, Franciscan sandals, the doors of perception, natural lifestyle, free sex, we're all authentic. Yes, a counterweight was needed, or else the system would crush everyone, as it had done time and again. There was something out of sync in this supposedly personal mission, but he didn't know it yet, adrift in an obstinately makeshift life. My life hasn't begun yet, he liked to say, as if justifying his own incompetence. So many years dedicated to ... to what was it now? To literature, to poetry, to an alternative lifestyle, to creation, to something bigger that he couldn't put his finger on — so many years and no results! Being alone was a good alibi. Living in a city with aggressive geniuses on every corner, he thought about the meagreness of his short stories, finally published, in which he found flaws every time he turned a page. The book of juvenile fiction published nationwide was to end with its first edition, after a stupid tiff with his editor in São Paulo a few months later. 'We need to cut this paragraph from the second edition because country school teachers are complaining.' He gave up on the book.

He still didn't know it, but he already sensed that it wasn't his niche. Three months earlier he'd finished *The Lyrical Terrorist*, and something better, still formless, seemed to be starting there. Someone struggling to free himself of his guru's influence, trying to leave the world of messages and enter the world of perception, guided by cold reason. He was no longer a poet. He'd lost forever his sense of the sublime, which, hackneyed as it may sound, was the fuel needed to write poetry. An idea of the sublime wasn't enough, he was beginning to realise — it only led to imitation.

He needed the strength and courage to summon the language of the world without sliding into the ridiculous. There's something incompatible between me and poetry, he told himself defensively. To assume poetry, it seemed, was to assume a religion, and he'd always been completely devoid of religious sentiment. A creature moving in the desert, he might have written, with some pomp, to describe his own solitude. Solitude as a mission, not a cause for sadness. I've never really managed to be on my own, he concluded, with a pang of anxiety. And now, he thought, instinctively glancing at the swinging doors, I never will. He'd recently started writing a new novel, *Essay on Passion*, in which, he imagined, he'd go through his life with a fine-tooth comb. And everyone else's, with a satirical tongue. No one would be spared. Three chapters ready. It was a cheerful book, he thought. I need to *begin* once and for all, he told himself, and it was only by writing that he'd discover who he was. Or so he hoped. There were too many things to organise, but, perhaps precisely for this reason, he felt good, happy, peopled with plans.

Suddenly, the doctor (whom he'd never liked and thus of whom he had no expectations) opened the swinging doors, unsmiling as always. There was nothing new about his lack of smile, which is why he, a kid father, barely managing to hide his flask of whisky, paid no heed. The man was removing his green gloves as if he'd just finished an unpleasant task. For some reason, it was this absurd image, no doubt false, that he retained of that moment.

'How are you?' he asked the doctor, because it's what you do. His mind was already a month down the track, seven months, a year and three months, five years … his child growing, his spitting image.

'It's a boy.'

No surprise either. I knew it was going to be the son of spring, he would have said, if he'd spoken.

'Your wife is fine.' And the doctor disappeared back where he'd come from.

He fell asleep, or almost fell asleep, on a red sofa next to the high hospital bed where they'd brought his wife at some point during the night. The baby was in the nursery, a kind of sterile cage that reminded him of *Brave New World*: all those babies side by side behind a protective window, labelled and registered for their entry into the world, all identical, bundled up in the same green clothes, all more or less ugly, all crumpled, little scares that breathed, all unmoving, absurdly fragile, all a tabula rasa, each of them a mere smidgen of potential, now eternally condemned to Brazil and the Portuguese language, which would lend them the words with which, one day, they would try to say who they were, after all, and why they were here, if indeed such a question can make sense.

Which one was his? That one there, the helpful nurse pointed, and he smiled as he looked at the unmoving baby, seeking a point of convergence — something external that would touch him suddenly, like an angel's finger. But no, he smiled, invincible — the point had to be created, it didn't just fall from heaven. A child was the idea of a child, and the idea he had was a good one. A good start. But its presence was also a birth back to front, because now — he might have thought, expelled from paradise — I'm on the other side of the glass. I'm no longer the baby in the cradle — it's not me over there anymore, and he laughed, almost drunk, his bottle empty, inebriated from the cigarettes he was smoking back to back in those tolerant times. It was as if, in a very prosaic manner, he'd merely lost a privilege — his freedom. Which was a word that, while it objectively meant a lot (that is, being in prison, being out of prison; being able to say and write anything or not being able to say or write anything — those were the last days of a dictatorship), subjectively, in another sphere, it was illusory. Sometimes it was enough. Being free meant being alone. Of course, there was his wife, for whom he nurtured a keen passion that even he had been slow to grasp (he'd never been quick on the uptake), but at the same time he needed to spend a lot of time on himself, patch together all those misshapen pieces of insecurity, such a pathetically incomplete kid, in order to take a better look at her, which he'd only manage to do years later. There was his wife, but they hadn't been born together. They could part ways, and the order of the universe would remain the same. But a child was another birth: he couldn't part ways with it. All the words that the new father had absorbed over the course of his life had instilled this consenting servitude in him, the brief but powerful ethical imperative that was created around so little: who is that baby there? What do we have in common? When all is said and done, did I have any choice? How can I reconcile the fundamental idea of individual freedom, which moves the fantastic wheel of the West, he declaimed, with the savagery of raw nature, which, through an inextricable succession of chance happenings, has now brought me this child? Rousseau himself abandoned his children, he remembered, enjoying himself. *Brave New World* was so much better, the sterility of birth without pain or parents. We live in each other's pockets, but instead of feeling nauseated at the thought (the invincible stickiness of human relationships), he smiled as he looked at the little gurgling bundle with a crumpled face behind the glass: it struck him as good and beautiful, the son of spring. He remembered the date: the small hours of the third of November, 1980.

He finally awoke from a disrupted but happy night's sleep (or had it been just a few minutes?), and he felt a pleasant kind of gravity in his movements, shaky from a kind of rebirth. Or displacement, he thought, almost physical — he wasn't in his habitual place anymore. Nor would he ever be again, he decided, always ready for irrevocable, lofty-sounding conclusions, good on the podium — it was a definitive, permanent, inevitable displacement. And that was a good thing, he concluded. Words. What time was it? His wife appeared to be asleep in a bed that looked more like an altar, a contraption of levers. He would like contraptions his whole life — he was a watchmaker. He took a moment to work out how the thing worked. A crank in the prow, like a Model T Ford, hoisted it up or down. A nurse came and went — there weren't many smiles, but that's how the machine worked, with precise efficiency. He timidly approached his wife, whose eyes were already open and tranquil, fearing she might be expecting some kind of sentimental or amorous outpouring from him, which always made him feel awkward, defensive. Dealing with emotion had never been his forte. He preferred the softness of humour to the ridiculousness of love, but he didn't know this yet, his legs too weak for the burden of his soul.

Her hand was warm.

'How are you?'

'Fine,' she said. 'It still hurts a bit. Has the doctor been yet?'

'No.'

Birth is a natural brutality, the obscene expulsion of the baby, the physical undoing of the mother to the limits of her resistance, the weight and fragility of living flesh, blood. A whole world of signs is created to conceal the thing itself, as primitive as a dark cave.

'Did you call the families?' she asked, smiling for the first time.

The families. Families were a pain in the neck, but a necessary, or inevitable, pain in the neck, which was the same thing at the end of the day. Now I'll have my own, he thought. Enough with the fighting. Only Arabs and Jews are able to stay at war all their lives, and he laughed at his joke, almost telling his wife, then changed his mind.

'I'll call them now. What time is it?' As if she could know.

When he walked into the corridor, he discovered that they'd already hung a little blue doll on the door and, absurdly, he thought about money, then reassured himself. Everything was fine. In the public cage of the newborns, he tried to recognise his son. There was a row of identical beings behind the glass, but he didn't seem to be there. What name would they give him? They'd chosen Alice for a girl, Felipe for a boy. Felipe. A fine name. As sharp as a knight against the horizon. A name with well-defined contours. Simple, self-evident dignity, he fantasised: Felipe. He repeated the name several times over, almost out loud, to make sure it didn't wear out with use, that it didn't crumble in its own sound, drained by the echo — Felipe, Felipe, Felipe, Felipe. No, it remained intact on the horizon, steady on its horse, a lance in its right hand. Felipe. Some grandparents next to him smiled, pointing at someone without a name, and also smiled at him, sharing his cheer — birth was a collective happiness. Humans really were all brothers and sisters, so similar to one another! He returned the smile, said a shy 'Congratulations,' and moved away for fear they might ask him something. He needed to make phone calls — the world was big, it needed to know the big news, and he didn't have any phone tokens. He was greeted with more smiles at reception, and bought some tokens at the booth there. Being civilised, he refrained from asking to call from the actual reception desk, where there was a telephone within arm's reach. Precisely so people wouldn't ask, there was a sign saying *TOKENS HERE*, and on the pavement outside was a row of public phones, one with its receiver ripped out and a pathetic dangling wire.

First he went for a good walk, to breathe deeply. It was a cool, beautiful morning, the slightest mist promising a day of clear, blue skies, and he tried once again to organise his day, his week, his month, his year, and his life. Now there's no turning back, which is good, he thought, and smiled at the cliché: the gate to the past closes; the gate to the future opens. His feeling of inferiority was still heavy; he made up for it with a parochial, stubborn, obtuse, sometimes cowardly pride, which he skilfully dressed up in humour. He knew himself. He'd often thought that there was no turning back, but there always had been. Under the streetlight on the corner, which was still a faint glow against the light of the day, he remembered his absurd adolescence, sniffing hallucinogens in Curitiba's public squares, just to hear a buzzing in his soul and see the phantasmagoric lights of the night multiplying in a psychedelic echo. The drone had once lasted for two days and he, fatherless, had decided to stop just from the fright. Yes, he'd managed to stop because he wasn't a street kid. At fifteen he had a good school, home, mother, family — and a desire to turn the world inside out. Now, and he smiled, holding the token, now he was on the right side of the world, already feeding the self-irony with which he defended himself from what would be his own downfall. A man of the system. Family was system. Fifty years from now, he imagined, without actually believing it, there will be no more families, and the world will be better. For now, we forge on with the weapons we have. His tone was already slightly ironic.

'Yes, just a little while ago! It's a boy! I don't know how much he weighs yet! He looks plump! I didn't tell anyone because it wasn't necessary.' He almost added, with a pang of pre-irritation: *That's all I needed, to wait for my son to be born with the rellies all milling around!* The idea was enough to satisfy him and he went on, politely. 'It was the middle of the night — why bother everyone? Yes. Yes! Come! Felipe! Nice, isn't it? She's great! Thanks! We need to celebrate!'

Across the street was a bar and restaurant with an enormous sign saying *Fried Chicken*. Employees were dragging rubbish bins out to the sidewalk, making a crazy racket; the day was beginning. He thought about going straight up to the counter and asking for a beer before they were even open, but he dismissed the stupid idea. As he walked back up the ramp to his wife's room, he glanced at his watch and once again saw the day of the month on which his son had been born: three, as if it contained a secret. He found his wife sleeping peacefully, and suddenly felt the brutality of his tiredness — he shouldn't have told anyone. Soon the relatives would start their harassment. He glanced at his watch again and calculated how long he had. It wasn't enough for the desire he felt, his eyes drooping, as though the weight of another being was pulling him down. He lay down on the awkward red sofa, too short for his legs, which suddenly reminded him of a moment lost in childhood. He saw the light overhead, missing one of its bulbs, closed his eyes, and fell asleep.

The most brutal morning of his life started with interrupted sleep — the relatives were arriving. He was visibly happy: a rather groggy happiness due to his lack of sleep, plus the shots of whisky, the intensity of the event, the series of little oddities in that official space that wasn't his. Once again he wasn't at home, and now there was an alienation in everything, as if it were he, rather than his wife, who'd pushed the child out of his very guts. The inevitable, good feeling started to give way to an invisible anguish that seemed to breathe with him. Perhaps he, like some women in the shock of childbirth, didn't want the child he had; but the idea was just a shadow. After all, he was just an unemployed man, and now he had a child. Period. It was no longer just an idea, nor the mere desire to please that his poem, the ridiculous 'Son of Spring', represented — it was an absence of everything. But the relatives were full of cheer, all babbling over one another. The tension of waking up in a daze was fading by the minute.

What does he look like? I don't know; he's all crumpled. He said what people always say about newborns to get a laugh, and it worked. He's a big, bouncing baby boy. He made it up. It was what they wanted to hear. Yes, everything's fine. Everyone needs to see him, but I think there are visiting hours. He'll be here soon — a little bundle of sighs. His wife was placid in the hospital bed — yes, yes, everything's fine. There was a laundry list of advice all at once. Everyone had something crucial to say about a newborn, especially to idiot dads like himself. I took a course for dads, he warned, clowning with them. But it was true. He'd spent an afternoon in a large circle of big-bellied women — his wife included, of course — with two or three other devoted future fathers, keenly listening to a basic lecture from a kindly doctor, and the only thing he could remember from it all was a single piece of advice: it was wise to stay on good terms with one's mother-in-law because parents sometimes needed a break from their kids, to get out for dinner from time to time, to try to recapture a little of the feel of how things used to be that was never coming back.

And the families talked and made suggestions (teas, herbs, remedies, infusions, what to do with milk). He needs a smack to make him cry out loud as soon as he's born, someone said, and someone else said no, the world's changed, and smacking a baby is stupid (though they didn't use this word). Aren't they going to bring him? What time was he born? What did the doctor say? What about you — what did you do? What happened? Why didn't you say anything beforehand? Why didn't you call anyone? What if something had gone wrong? Has he got a name yet? Yes: Felipe. The relatives were in high spirits, but he was suddenly tired, and felt a pang of his old, insoluble anxiety creeping back. He wanted to go home once and for all and rebuild a good routine, because he'd soon have books to write. I'd like to delve into *Essay on Passion* again, he thought. Anything to get out of here, out of this small makeshift world. Yes, and have a beer, of course! Now, that's a good idea — and he almost glanced about for some company so he could really talk about this day, organise this day, think about it, literally, as a rebirth. Look, my life has a new meaning now, he'd say, weighing his words. I need to discipline myself so I can establish a new routine and survive in peace with my dream. A child is like — and he smiled, alone, the idiot, amidst the relatives — like a certificate of authenticity, he'd venture; and he floated off again in a Rousseauian dream of communion with nature, which had never really been his own but which he'd absorbed like a mantra and was afraid to let go of — without that one last link, what was left? Everywhere else, other people had authority, not him. The only free territory is that of literature, he might have theorised, had he managed to think about it. Yes, he needed to call his old guru, to somehow get his blessing. Many years later, a student would tell him, in writing, why he wasn't given to intimacy. 'You give others the impression you're always on the defensive.' Primal feelings tumbled over one another — he still didn't understand a thing, but life was good. He still didn't know that here began a different marriage with his wife because of the simple fact that they had had a child together. He didn't know anything yet.

Suddenly the door opened and two doctors, the paediatrician and the obstetrician, came in, and one of them was holding a bundle. They were surprisingly serious, absurdly serious, heavy, for such a happy moment. They looked like generals. There were about ten people in the room, and his wife was awake. It was an abrupt entry, violent even. With quick, decisive steps, they each went to one side of the bed, where they stood, erect. His wife watched as her child was deposited before her like an offering, but no one smiled. They came like high priests. In times past, one of them would have brought down his dagger in one fell swoop to spill the creature's guts and tear out the future. Five seconds of silence. Everyone froze — a sudden, electric, brutal, paralysing tension pierced their souls — while one of the doctors unwrapped the baby on the bed. These were the stages of a ritual that was created instantaneously, with its own gestures and rules, which were immediately respected. Everyone waited.

There was the beginning of a speech, almost religious, which he, reeling, couldn't grasp except in fragments of the paediatrician's voice.

'... certain characteristics ... important signs ... look. See the eyes, the fold of skin in the inside corner of the eyelid, the slant ... the little finger curved inwards ... the back of the cranium is flatter ... muscular hypotonia ... the lower-set ears and ...'

He immediately remembered his friend's master's thesis in genetics. He'd proofread it two months earlier, and the characteristics of trisomy 21 (known as Down syndrome, or, more crudely, back in the 1980s, 'mongolism'), the subject of the thesis, were still fresh in his mind. He and his friend had discussed several aspects of the thesis and curiosities of the study (one that suddenly sprang to mind was the first question an Arabic family had asked when told of the problem: 'Will he be able to have children?' Which seemed funny, like another cartoon). Thus, in a split second, in the biggest delirium of his life — the only one, strictly speaking, that he didn't have the time, and wouldn't have for the rest of his life, to domesticate in a literary representation — he learned the power of the expression 'forever': the idea that some things really were irremediable, and the absolute, but obvious feeling that there was no turning back time, which was something he'd always refused to accept. Once, everything could be started over, but not now; everything could be redone, but not this; everything could go back to nothing and be remade, but now everything had a granite-like, insurmountable solidity. The last frontier, that of innocence, had been crossed. His stubbornly prolonged childhood ended here. Feeling faint to his very core, reeling backwards, not hearing another word of the doctors' stupid babble, he remembered the thesis that he'd read line by line, painstakingly correcting syntactical and stylistic details here and there, amused by the curiosities that described, with the cold, exact power of science, his child's essence. Which was this word: 'mongoloid'.

He refused to advance on the timeline, struggling to stay in the second before the revelation, like a cow bucking in the narrow aisle of the slaughterhouse. He refused to look at the bed, where everyone else had trained their gaze in brute silence, gaping at the unexpected curse. This is worse than anything else, he realised. Not even death has this power to destroy me. Death calls for seven days of grieving, and then life goes on. But not now. This will never end. He took two, three steps backwards until he bumped into the red sofa and looked out the window, to the other side, upwards, in a bovine refusal to see and hear. It wasn't tears of sorrow that were building up, but something mixed with a furious kind of hatred. He was unable to fully turn against his wife, which was perhaps his first impulse and first alibi (he still refused to look at her). Something, some shred of civility, curbed his urge to be violent, and at the same time he felt a deep certainty, which was both revenge and an escape valve (the truly scientific certainty, he remembered, as if raising an irrefutable trump card to show the world: I know, I've read about it, I don't need your stories), that the only correlation that could be established about the causes of mongolism, the only proven variable, was the mother's age and hereditary predisposition. Also, immersed in the same suffering with no exit, gazing at the blue sky on the other side of the window, he remembered how some years earlier they had sought genetic counselling about the possibility of their children inheriting (if the gene was dominant or recessive) his wife's retinal degeneration — a serious, but bearable visual limitation that had stabilised when she was a child. Denial. He refused to look at the bed, at his son, at his wife, at the relatives, at the doctors — he felt terribly ashamed of his son, and was certain he'd feel the vertigo of hell every minute of his life from then on. No one was prepared for their first child, he tried to think, defensively, much less a child like this: something he simply couldn't transform into a son.

When he finally turned to look at the bed, there was no one left in the room — just himself, his wife, and the child in her arms. He couldn't bring himself to look at his son. Yes, his soul was still bucking, looking for a solution, since he couldn't turn the clock back five minutes. But no one was condemned to be what they were, he realised, as if he had seen the philosopher's stone: I don't need this child, he thought, and it was as if the idea put him on his feet again, albeit stumbling step by step into darkness. I don't need this wife either, he almost added, in a mental dialogue without a listener. As always, he was alone.

A silent network of solidarity — the solidarity of tragedy, a taciturn solidarity — formed around him in a matter of hours, but he didn't want to listen to anyone. He was still bucking; the next minute of his life was in front of him, but he didn't want to open the door. In the silence with his wife and child, he found himself crying, but it didn't last long. He desperately tried to find a word in that emptiness; there wasn't one. It was hard to bring his gaze to rest on anything — like the thing in his wife's arms, his wife to whom he couldn't find anything to say. A tiny breath of civilisation made him touch her hands — an empty, false gesture, cold as ice — while his eyes danced across the white walls, looking for a way out. He had to find something to say, but he never knew what. Many years earlier, when graduating from junior high, he'd tried to write a speech to run for the position of class speaker, which would have made him visually prominent, up there on the podium, but he hadn't got past the first exhortation: Fellow classmates! His arm made the gesture, his tone of voice was good, his posture appropriate: Fellow classmates! But his soul plummeted into a void. Words grew on trees, all he had to do was reach out and there they were, but he was absurdly incapable of finding a single one that was appropriate. Now, again, the same feeling. Fellow classmates!

As he sometimes did in unpleasant moments, he fast-forwarded through his own future, the vertiginous passage of time, things happening fatally one after another, ageing and death, then voila, it was over, a delirious cartoon, a succession of drawings. What was this moment compared to everything else that was, perhaps, already written for him? An insignificant moment in the life of an insignificant person worried about another insignificant being — just a statistic. Go to any maternity ward, and for every one thousand births there will be, like in a lottery, a child with Down syndrome, and this will feed other statistics and studies such as the one he had proofread, his curiosity piqued.

There were so many things between heaven and earth! Cretinous children, in the technical sense of the word — children who'd never attain half the intelligence quotient of a normal person; who'd have practically no autonomy; who'd be incapable of abstraction, the miracle that defines us; and whose notion of time wouldn't go much beyond an immemorial, millennial yesterday and a nebulous tomorrow. For them, time didn't exist. Speech would forever be a babble of single words and short, truncated sentences; they'd be incapable of producing a phrase in the passive voice (*the window was broken by João* would be beyond their comprehension). Their footsteps would always be uncertain and slow, and if their parents didn't keep an eye on them, they'd grow as fat as barrels, propelled by a hunger unchecked by a feeling of fullness, which was neurologically tardy. Everything about them was tardy. They were short-sighted; their world exasperatingly small. The only things that existed for them were those at hand. They were obstinate, stubborn, and had a hard time controlling their impulses, which were circular and repetitive. They'd only learn to walk long after the normal period. And they were ugly, short children, almost dwarves — little, open-mouthed ogres with big tongues and flat necks, wide as tree trunks. In just a few minutes (he didn't think it, but that was what was happening), this horrible child had already occupied every pore of his life. He would be joined to it for the rest of time by an invisible, ten-to-twelve-metre rope. Then a sliver of light suddenly appeared to him, something else he remembered from the thesis he'd proofed, and, that morning, after a poor night's sleep, barely awoken from a nightmare, the idea (or fact — scientific actually, thus indisputable) struck him as his salvation. Freedom!

It was as if it had already happened — he let go of his wife's hands and abruptly left the room in a stupid, intense euphoria that swept his soul. He needed to savour this truth, this scientific fact, deeply: yes, children with Down syndrome died young. By some mystery of that jumble of excessive enzymes in someone who had three chromosome 21s instead of just two like everyone else, mongoloid children (the monstrous word now took on the sterile touch of scientific jargon — just its cold definition, not its prejudice) were abnormally susceptible to infections. A simple cold could quickly lead to pneumonia and then death — sometimes it was just a question of hours, he calculated. And there was more, he rejoiced: most of them had serious heart problems, congenital malformations, which gave them a very short life expectancy. Extremely short, he repeated, as if teaching a class, shaking his head from side to side compassionately. It's sad, but true. Did you all write that down? And there were thousands of other tiny manufacturing defects. A car wouldn't be able to drive like that. He lit another cigarette, and it seemed as if his whole life was returning to normal when he felt that wonderful draught of intense, perfumed smoke. See, he told himself, there are no old mongoloids. Are you sure about that? someone would ask, raising a hand. Yes, absolutely … they die young. And he wanted to stroll down a bustling street at six in the evening just to verify *in loco*, head by head, this indisputable truth: they don't exist. See for yourself. Search the crowd: they don't exist. It was almost midday, and the maternity ward was busy. A nurse asked him something and he said no, he was on his way out, not wanting to think too much about his discovery for fear of spoiling it, to better enjoy the freedom that suddenly lay before him. Perhaps, he calculated, it was only a matter of days, depending on the gravity of the syndrome.

There are no mongoloids in history; there are no reports of them — they are absent beings. Read Plato's dialogues, medieval narratives, *Don Quixote*, go forward to Balzac's *The Human Comedy*, then Dostoyevsky, and not even he — always concerned with the humiliated and downtrodden — mentions them. Mongoloids don't exist. Not because of historical persecution, or prejudice, he thought, lighting another cigarette (it was a beautiful day, the almost chilly morning mist had already dissipated, and the sky was delightfully blue, the blue sky of Curitiba, which, when it appeared, he thought, drifting off, was one of the best in the world), but simply because they didn't have any natural defences. They only appeared late in the twentieth century. In the whole of *Ulysses*, in the course of those twenty-four full-on hours, James Joyce didn't have Leopold Bloom run into a single child with Down syndrome. Thomas Mann completely ignores them. The film industry, in its eighty-year history, he thought, straining to remember, had never featured them. Nor would it. Mongoloids were hospital creatures, forever in doctors' waiting rooms. Few lived more than … how many years? About ten, he thought, then compared it to his own age, and thought it was a lot. Maybe five, he fantasised, and he immediately saw a rapid sequence of years, his friends concerned with his struggle, hands patted his shoulder, but it was no good — the boy died yesterday. No, he didn't make it. They'd return from the cemetery with the tragedy weighing on their souls, but life begins again, after all, doesn't it? A breath of renewal — as if he'd existed merely to give them strength, to unite them, mother and father, sacred. He saw himself walking through Barigüi Park, perhaps on a beautiful, melancholic morning like this one, thinking over those five or three years, maybe two. The mettle of the soul — that was the expression with which to start his speech. Fellow classmates! We need mettle!

Why worry? Having taken refuge in the crystalline truth that his son wouldn't live long (it was just a kind of trial that God, if he existed, had placed in his life to test his mettle, as he had done with Job), the world seemed to reorganise itself completely. He'd always been optimistic — a man of the twentieth century, in love with technology, enthused by the idea of pleasure, fascinated by women, attracted by intelligence, immersed in the world of words, impregnated by two or three basic ideas of humanism and freedom, a little Pangloss from the province, in rapid transformation. At the same time, a tentacular network of relationships, of which he would never completely free himself, seemed to hold him back and immobilise him. I have no competence for survival, he concluded. I've never held down a regular job in my life. I think I'm a writer, but I still haven't written anything. All I have is a newborn child who will probably die soon. But this, this near death (he gagged, trying not to think about it, lighting another cigarette, trying to recover the thread of a routine that simulated normality; what to do now, have lunch?), this fact, this death foretold, struck him at that moment as the only good thing in his life.

Just like in his imaginary cartoon, in which events followed one another without interruption, he was back at home. There was a semblance of normality, from the blue doll on the door of his son's room (the presents, the packages, the hanging rattles, the decorations, the incredible paraphernalia of a newborn, nappies, talc, clothes, tiny shoes, frills, toys) to all the other little details. He and his wife talked to one another as if nothing had changed, until a small surge of depression gripped one of them, and then some gesture from the other restored whatever normality was possible, bringing the scales back into balance. The idea, or hope, that the baby would die soon secretly reassured him. He never shared this liberating revelation with his wife. In one of his recurring fantasies, he embraced and consoled her over their son's tragic death from a sudden fever. But she was well aware of the risk, and worked in the opposite direction; in those first few days she was constantly, obsessively alert to the smallest sign of anything that might pose a threat to her son. Who, as it happened, looked very healthy for a baby with his genetic make-up. He opened his awful mouth and cried a lot, and when he slept, he slept too much. He needed to be woken up, someone suggested. The more he moved, the better. Better for whom? he wondered. He moved like any other baby. His tongue seemed a little longer than other children's, but babies were ductile creatures. They formed and deformed easily, taking on different contours daily. When he put his finger in the baby's palm, the infant gripped it with some strength, which, they said, was a sign of good health. But his head, he thought, is too big, even for babies, who are naturally big-headed. That neck. And that shrill crying — is that normal?

No, nothing would ever be normal in his life again until the end of time. He was beginning to feel for the first time, in his soul, the agony of normality. He'd never really been normal. His notion of normality had crumbled many years earlier, when his father died. Everything he'd done since then had steered him away from any form of it, but, at the same time, he ardently yearned to be recognised and admired by others. Which, if you thought about it, was absolutely normal, he might have said now. A typical child, a typical teenager. A typical adult? He was a mixture of ideology and inadequacy, dream and incompetence, desire and frustration, lots of reading and no perspective. Everything seemed more like his own little pantomime than something concrete, because he had taken few risks, afraid of the very solitude that he nourished daily. All of his projects were only half-finished: his attempt to become a merchant navy officer, his watchmaking, his involvement in the Rousseauian actors' community, his dependence on a guru who could do no wrong, his self-sufficient Nietzschean arrogance with fascist touches from those happy times (he now realised), and finally the debacle of surrendering to a formal marriage by signing those ridiculous papers in an even more ridiculous event, dressed in a coat (but not a tie, he'd held out — no tie!), his lack of direction, his stupid unwillingness to break with his own past, a shipwreck of himself, then his university degree with its definitive induction into the system without any of its advantages, insubordinately unemployed, a writer without a book, moving in the slippery shadow of his good humour — and now a father without a son.

He needed to face things as they were; he needed to disarm himself. To not avoid the awful weight of the present. The whole philosophy of this century rests on this empty instant, he mused. The problem is that things (his son now, and the whole endless, asphyxiating sum of tiny, everyday facts that he'd accumulated all his life with the feeling that he was creating and nourishing his own personality) aren't anything in themselves. The world doesn't speak. I'm the one who lends it my words; I'm the one who says what things are. This is an unparalleled power — I can falsify everything and everyone, always, a narcissistic Midas, making everything in my own image, desire, and likeness. Which is more or less what everyone does all the time: falsify. This monumental gibberish everywhere, everyone saying everything at every instant, this collective fear of silence. Is there another perspective? Nothing has any essence (he remembered the books he'd read) anywhere. Now that makes sense. I just need to escape this asphyxia. A son is as close as you can get to the idea of destiny, to that which you don't escape. Or is it that which you can't escape? Why not? Why can't I choose another path? (That was a question he'd ask himself many times throughout life.) Because I already have an essence, he answered, which I made myself. My freedom is a very narrow strip, just wide enough for me to stand in.

In the dark, the baby slept.

He lit a cigarette in the living room. It was a rare moment of calm; but, straining his ears, he heard his wife crying in the bedroom, almost the crying of a shy child. He remained static, listening. The baby wasn't taking the breast — it was a major fuss just for him to get a few drops of milk. The doctors recommended a contraption, which pleased him, of course — a small glass funnel with a rubber pump. A delicate object, it reminded him of something old, a pharmacy in a film, a medieval alchemist. It extracted milk like a da Vinci invention, he thought. Yellowy drops — it didn't look like milk. Tense days for his wife, he knew. In the midst of a crisis, in a desperate wail, she had said, 'I've ruined your life.' And he hadn't answered, as if agreeing, his hand stroking her hair to console her suffering, not the truth of the facts. Perhaps she's right, he thought now, in the dark of the living room. Best not to falsify anything. She's ruined my life — he took refuge in the hollowness of the phrase, feeling its echo, and this gave him some comfort.

Normality. What was he to tell other people when he saw them? Yes, my son's been born. Yes, everything's fine. That is, he's mongoloid. No, it was too heavy a word. And no one in Brazil had heard of 'Down syndrome' in 1980. The polite thing to say was: Yes, he has a small problem. He has mongolism. But that required a whole set of subsequent explanations, and people never knew what to say or do in that awkward situation. To their concerned 'You don't say!' he'd give them a pat on the back, smile, and say, but it's OK, they're good-humoured children; with good treatment they can be practically normal. 'Practically normal.' What he wanted to resolve now wasn't the problem of his son, but the space he occupied in his life. And those hideous everyday brushes with others: having to explain. He had already seen in the encyclopaedia that the syndrome was named after the British physician John Langdon Haydon Down (1828–1896). In the British Empire's best scientific tradition, Down had been the first to describe it, stressing the similarities between sufferers' facial features and the Mongols, in a far-flung corner of Asia — hence 'mongoloids'. What kind of mentality led one to define a syndrome by comparing sufferers' facial features to those of an ethnic group? It was a case of the Englishman as the measure of all things. Prince Charles, that Apollonian figure, was the standard of racial normality. He laughed in the dark, lighting another cigarette. And how had this designation come to last more than a century, as if it was something normal and acceptable? Yes, normal and acceptable, even to himself. He remembered now, a shiver running down his spine, how just a few weeks back he had commented on his lecturer's stupidity to a fellow classmate. 'She's like a mongoloid,' he'd said. The word had come to him easily, from the thesis he'd proofed. All he'd had to do was reach out a hand and pluck it off the tree. 'Don't spit into the wind.' He remembered the popular expression, with its shrewd, pragmatic wisdom, always seeking a secret justice in everything so as to sidestep the terrible fact of chance that defined us.

The problem of normality. Maybe he'd write a short script of the things people should say when he confessed the tragedy. Something like, 'You don't say! But I imagine there are lots of resources these days, right? Look, if there's anything I can do, let me know,' to which he'd reply, 'Thank you, everything's fine.' Then they'd change the subject and that would be it. In many encounters he wouldn't need to say anything. There were billions of people who didn't know him, as opposed to some ten or twelve who did, and they already knew; nothing else needed to be said. In most cases it was enough to say, 'Yes, the baby's fine. His name's Felipe. Thanks.' And nothing more would be asked and nothing more would be answered; that would be the end of the matter, and life would go on as always. He sighed with relief.

The problem was that there wasn't really a place for this

child in his life. He remembered, in panic, the poem 'The Son of Spring', which suddenly struck him as completely ridiculous, pathetic: his dread of bad texts, of bad taste, of supreme kitsch came crashing down on his head and in his memory. He'd submitted it for publication in the literary magazine, and now he started to sweat just thinking about it. He'd have to bear it in print — someone might even come up and congratulate him on his talent and sensibility. 'You've dealt with the problem so well!' they'd say in solidarity, with a strong handshake, a smile of admiration. Yes, everyone always knew he had talent. And the blatant lie: a corny poem for a retarded child. He had to stop it from being published. He lost all trace of drowsiness just thinking about it. I'll talk to the magazine editor, first thing tomorrow, he thought. 'Please don't publish my poem. There's still time, isn't there?' He still didn't know it, but all it had taken was a tiny dose of hard reality to refine his sense of literature. But here the problem was something else.

Shame. Shame, he would say later, is one of the most powerful tools of social control. It makes us look for the degree of normality in each everyday gesture. Don't get out of line. Don't go crazy. And, above all, don't do anything ridiculous. He sincerely believed he'd overcome that obstacle once and for all — the theatre group he'd participated in years earlier, the actors' community, that pretentious grandiloquence masquerading as street theatre, had already yielded him enough embarrassment for a PhD in cheek. But there he'd had the protection of the group and the shield of not giving a damn — he could still be anything at any time; he could still change tack; he had no destiny at all. All he had was the happy arrogance of freedom. Fuck everyone.

The Kennedy family had hidden a retarded child from the world for its whole life. There was a lot at stake, it was true — but the biggest motivation was shame. Shame controlled everyone from dustmen to presidents. It was a powerful key to everyday life. 'Those politicians should be ashamed!' we tell ourselves every day, mouthing a mantra that redeems and tranquillises us. As if it was the same thing, he now felt shame, although the word, curiously, didn't stir anything in him, the sound of the word in its simplicity. It was as if something so absurdly simple — shame — couldn't be part of his life. Only the mediocre feel shame, he told himself. What he felt under his skin, what burned, was the unbearable feeling that something was wrong. And not that something was wrong with his son, but with himself.

The baby was asleep now; his wife, too, and he lit another cigarette, in the dark. She was right: she'd ruined his life. He sighed, agreeing, and mysteriously felt calmer.

In just two days another powerful hypothesis appeared, enabling him to shrug off the weight of the present: that the diagnosis was wrong and the baby was actually normal or had some other kind of problem, much less serious.

There was only one way to be sure: to do a karyotype analysis, a photograph of the chromosomes. But he couldn't fool himself. He knew it was a remote possibility — the boy was like a living demonstration of all the syndrome's most obvious characteristics, practically a textbook example that could be used in a classroom. In a conversation with his genetics-expert friend, he had discovered the possibility of a miraculous — though strictly scientific — salvation. A few years earlier, a French researcher investigating the occurrence of trisomy in twins had discovered that there could be a partial manifestation of the syndrome. His study revealed that a specific part of the extra chromosome was solely responsible for the mental retardation, and another segment, also highly specific, was responsible for the physical appearance, or phenotype — the set of external characteristics that made diagnosis possible. In the case of the twins, a fortuitous example, the problem had been 'distributed'. One of them, whose appearance was perfectly normal, presented the mental deficiency typical of the syndrome, while the other, whose appearance was unequivocally that of a child with Down syndrome, was mentally normal.

The case was a miracle (a chance occurrence that the researcher had been lucky to catch), but the father clung to the miracle the minute he heard about it. Yes, there was practically do doubt that Felipe was a normal child. Look how he grips your finger as soon as you touch his palm! Most probably, he argued, worked up, perhaps so as not to hear himself speaking, most probably the only part of the chromosome affected was the one that determined physical characteristics, not the one responsible for mental retardation. This fantasy gave him the stamina to survive another few days, skipping ahead in visionary lapses that he himself found funny, nervously worrying about the child's ugliness — how could he convince others that the little monster was, in fact, a normal child? The other, more solid, hypothesis, that it was beyond a doubt a trisomy of chromosome 21, wouldn't have been such a tragedy either, after all, because of the baby's vulnerability — one infection, and it wouldn't survive. At any rate, Pangloss was happy! All he wanted was something he could quietly lean on at that moment, anything but to face the fact in itself. Let time slip past, in the limbo of the subconscious. Once again he would come out at the other end, alone, safe and sound, more experienced, more mature, more inwardly convinced of his great destiny.

It was necessary, however, to go through with the karyotype. Until the mid-1950s, the cause of 'mongolism' wasn't known. It was the French doctor Jerôme Lejeune (1926–1994) who first described the syndrome with a perfectly delimited genetic characteristic — the trisomy of chromosome 21. In 1958 (the father avidly read the material his friend had lent him), Lejeune went to Denmark to develop photos of chromosomes that he had taken in a French laboratory. Later, in Canada, he presented his theory of 'chromosomal determinism' in 'mongoloids'. The following year, he published his work, demonstrating, for the first time, the link between a chromosomal aberration and mental deficiency. It was another step towards the de-demonisation of the world, proving once again the absurd, arbitrary, erratic, random nature of the facts in this sensitive area (the privileged territory of magic, wizards, evil-eyes, curses, and other such esoteric fads). In short, a karyotype was in itself just another of life's demonstrations of the profound indifference of all things. He closed his eyes, trying to give his despair a cold dignity. The chance nature of living beings is a fact, he repeated, as if the revelation in itself could save him from the abyss. But he was still incapable of asking the next question: so what?

While they were at the hospital (he remembered now, lighting another cigarette and staring at the ceiling), his brother had come to visit him.

'You already knew,' his brother had said, serious as a priest, as if whispering an esoteric secret accessible only to initiates, leaning towards him like a first-century Christian in disguise, moving in the shadows of hostile paganism, and showed him the indisputable document — one of the ten poems he'd written years before, in a pension in Portugal, in his backpacking days, and sent to his brother. 'Everything is in everything,' he might have added. His brother had always refused to take any medicine, even with a fever of 42°C; at the most, some cold water on his forehead. 'Nature knows what it's doing.' He unfolded the piece of paper, already anticipating what was there. Irritated by the calm, medieval consolation his brother was offering, he reluctantly reread his own text:

Nothing that wasn't
could have been.
There is no other time
over this time.

Tomorrow and tomorrow
is a curved staircase.
No one opens the door
still a model
Today we hear the rats
gnawing at the other side.
No one has got there,
because today is here.

But dreams insist
dreams transport
dreams trace
a straight staircase.

When you cut the bread
What comes after tomorrow
is of no importance.
Although you know:
all forces
are united
so the new day will dawn.

He was too beaten down right then to argue back, but he
started to pick and brood over his own poem as soon as he was
alone. None of this is me, he said out loud. This is a simulacrum
of poetry; the verses fail to cover their tracks, in an elementary,

amateurish way. The 'nothing that wasn't' is a distant, inept echo of Eliot's *Four Quartets*, which in turn repeats Ecclesiastes, but my reference is false. I've never sat through a whole mass in my life. I don't know Latin, nor do I read the Bible. I don't like priests, pastors, prophets, rabbis, or miracle-workers. I suffer from an ingrained anti-clericalism. I have absolutely no time for this mythical causality that people want to invent in Western culture, these Styrofoam coats of arms, painted gold, that have come through time. I've never read Virgil all the way through; it's all wisdom from a sophisticated almanac. T. S. Eliot is incomprehensible to me. And he continued, almost out loud, 'Nothing that wasn't could have been': I inherited that triteness from my old guru, for whom there was a mysterious 'correct proportion' among all things. Yet another magical, medieval explanation of the world: 'everything is in everything' — a delirium that attracts, and tranquillises, so many millions of people every day. There is cause and blame in everything — and there has to be, there absolutely has to be a meaning for things, or we fall into the abyss. The father found the idea of randomness unbearable — because that was precisely where he wanted to be, in that which could not be born, as if he could leave his body and become an abstraction. The curved stairs of tomorrow, the door still a model, were echoes of a line from some poem by Carlos Drummond de Andrade that he'd read, repeated, and memorised so many millions of times since he was a child that they were already a part of his syntax. The final verse, reminiscent of a military march, came from some diffuse set of Marxist ideals, the language of the time, à la Cuban Revolution (comrades, rise up!), dialectical determinism, the idea that the absolute causality of nature was tied up with the contingent randomness of the facts of culture and history; socialist 'realism'. The 'forces united' were,

45

perhaps, a hand-me-down from some resounding line of grand birth. The desire for a new day to dawn, perhaps on a Saturday, had a little something of Vinicius de Moraes and Geraldo Vandré in it. And he remembered that the poem had been written in Portugal, in the middle of the Carnation Revolution — five interim governments in one year. He'd absorbed it through osmosis — and a little laziness. Paradise was near; he just had to work out the details.

A really big problem was the one he had now. His poetic self-destruction had left him reeling in the hospital corridor. But he knew exactly what he didn't want, and that was poetic comfort: he didn't want a crutch. I want the fact in itself — the essence of things — he mused, unable to resist the bravado of it. He wanted to keep his pride intact, the sense of superiority he'd so painstakingly nourished, which had always been his life's blind mission — either that or do nothing, be like everyone else, stamping forms behind a counter, sucking up to someone, depending on his own graciousness and the graciousness of others, asking favours, being the same as everyone else, in his incomplete understanding of things. All the crap, the rubbish he saw all around him. I don't want that. I've never wanted it, he thought. (Another parade of fantasies sprung to mind: the archetypes, the mythical figures of Greece, grandiose and kitsch, with its semi-naked gods, and the Fates, whom no one fought, since their destiny had already been written for them. It was the birth of tragedy, of Nietzsche, whose most powerful passages he had laboriously copied out in the sinister silence of the Coimbra Library.) No, his destiny lay elsewhere. The essence of things. Repeat it over and over, he told himself out loud, and see if it keeps its meaning. The essence of things. The essence of things.

The essence of things, at that moment, was Lejeune's

discovery, so simple in its prosaic laboratory methodology, in the complete lack of pathos of the best science, his ant-like work with little glass slides, for years on end. Truly unspectacular work. Mediocre. A hypothesis was posed and the hypothesis was tested; the operation was repeated until one arrived at the 'truth of things'. Yes, an apple could fall on one's head and one could have a moment of insight — the law of gravity — but it didn't eliminate the need for a hypothesis or its systematic testing. He knew it was swampy terrain and he knew it wasn't his. What was his terrain again? His pride was colossal, he was as stubborn as a mule, and he had a glowing awareness of his own destiny — as big as that of the Greeks — and solitude as an ethical value. But what did he have? Nothing. He was supported by his wife, he'd never written a really good text, he was deeply insecure, and now he had a son who — if he survived, which wasn't likely — would be a useless stone he'd have to drag uphill every morning, only to do it over the next day and so on until the end of time, like a little village Sisyphus. He wouldn't have the courage to kill him, to offer him to the gods as a sacrifice, which would give things the epic dimension of sacred times, he mused. He yearned for primordial purity; the brutality of the Dionysian world; tribal values. If someone as big as Heidegger was able to offer up his soul with such good will to the tribe, why couldn't he do the same? He laughed — the only good dimension he had at that moment was humour. He hid in its shadows. Laughter unravelled things — no tragedy survived it. And it hid things: he who laughs is not visible. Laughter is formless, creating an illusion of the universal equality of all things.

The essence. He repeated: the essence of things. With his wife and son, he approached the genetics building at the university. They had been there once before, years earlier, trying to assess the hereditary probability of his wife's suspected retinosis, whose characteristics were indecipherable. Newton Freire-Maia had classified it as a dominant gene — there was a 50 per cent chance that their children would get it. Listening to Freire-Maia, he remembered Mendel's laws, from back in high school. He remembered the perfect tree, geometrically delimiting blue eyes (a 25 per cent probability, depending on the parents) and brown eyes (a 75 per cent probability). He'd liked it. He *saw*, graphically, the power of possibility, drawing lines from here to there — recessive genes, dominant genes. It was an exact science. (Someone told him years later that Mendel had most probably forged his pea calculations to make the results so miraculously exact. It didn't matter. Mendel had arrived at the law, which still applied to every birth of all the billions in the world.) Fifty per cent? It was a reasonable wager against destiny; the power of passion, and he'd hugged his wife. What was 50 per cent? A mere idea. Yes, let's bet our chips on ourselves, on red — and they'd kissed and made love. But the roulette had backfired, it had stopped on black, the ball had shot off to another casino table, and now they had trisomy 21 in their arms.

They still needed to classify the type of trisomy. If it was a simple version, the chance of them having another child with the syndrome was minimal. If it was a different type, it wasn't so minimal. With smiles on their faces, the kind professors explained the mechanism of the chromosomes. He saw the enlarged black-and-white photograph, the numbered sequence of irregular pairs that looked like teeth with roots, out of focus. We're all there, he imagined. Come to think of it, there were few variables for so many preposterous results. Science organises. What comes scrambled in nature, science analyses and lays out in a row according to size and characteristics. This chromosome here, number 21 (and the professor pointed), came in greater numbers: there are three instead of two. If this is the case, it's clear. Besides … besides, the phenotype, the set of physical characteristics, doesn't contradict it. But.

A drop of blood. The baby barely moved, deep in the darkness of sleep. Then his parents' blood, but only in the name of science, to feed the genetic database. Perhaps some researcher, armed with the karyotypes of hundreds of parents of children with Down syndrome, would have a moment of insight and discover a new law of genetic recurrence. But he wasn't worried about that now — just the result to come. He was already perfectly inducted into his destiny in this first instance: I have a child with mongolism (he couldn't bring himself to say the word 'mongoloid' anymore), he told himself, and I have to deal with it. That's the problem. Don't invent any others. Not now. The initial shock from a few days earlier was beginning to wear off. Not least because he had an alternative destiny tucked away: the baby's fragility (the next moment, he tried to avoid thinking about it, shaking his head, but the idea was there) would take care of the rest. Faking consternation, he listened to the professors' statistics: approximately 80 per cent of mongoloid children didn't live very long. But things were changing quickly, they stressed. (Not in my case, he thought, and shook his head.) Maybe there really was a correct proportion among all things. But now, like a benched player who suddenly sees his chance to return to the game, there was another variable: what if the karyotype showed that he was a normal child? Just this ridiculous shred of hope gave him a few days of normality, until the test results were ready. Perhaps, he thought, as he returned to the open sky, to the beautiful day, I should keep working on my book and forget myself a bit.

They still needed to consult a medical-genetics specialist to see if Felipe had any heart problems — all the doctors had told them there was nothing wrong with his health, but the incidence of heart problems in children with trisomy 21 was very high. A specialist would know how to accurately locate it, if there was such a problem. As they crossed the courtyard of miracles in front of Hospital das Clínicas, they saw dirty, maimed, Christian poverty; the bedraggled all in a row; immemorial wretchedness begging for alms; and, here and there, ambulances arriving from other towns with potential voters who limped in on crutches, cattle chewing their cud and gazing at the counter, where there was an incomprehensible, insurmountable fence, tended by another breed of cattle who stamped forms and handed out numbers. Seventh heaven was a corridor that led to another room where an apostle in white placed a clean, white hand on heads to summon a miraculous cure — he thought of Nietzsche and his horror of pity, and how he embraced humiliation as a value, humility as a cause, poverty as greatness. But his son, should the tragedy be confirmed, wouldn't even make it to this point (he glanced around), because he wouldn't have the brains to invent a god who would give him strength, nor would he have the language to ask a favour.

What gave the father strength now, in the to-ing and fro-ing of those dreadful days, was precisely the perspective of his son's heart problem, which would quickly put an end to the nightmare, he fantasised, and once again he imagined himself receiving heartfelt hugs and condolences. He conjured up a vague image from an English film — a burial under a tree on a melancholic afternoon, everyone dressed in black, but without an accompanying religious service. A clean, calm ceremony. A new beginning: the world beginning with a sigh of relief. He couldn't shake the stupid death wish. He tried to suppress it (first the mirage of a genetic mistake, which would make this birth just a small prank of destiny), then felt ashamed of himself and the stupidity of his secret cold-bloodedness. But he was unable to suppress it; it came back in lapses, irresistible, like a dream.

The door opened and a polite young medical resident received them with a smile. She looked at the baby, sleeping softly in his mother's arms, with maternal endearment. They'd have to fill out some forms first, she explained in a friendly voice. He felt like an untamed animal, tossing his head to free himself of the bit in his mouth, an uncomfortable bridle tugging him back. Answering idiotic questions while sitting at a table, there was always an invasion of privacy (What do you do? How do you make a living? Who do you think you are?) and the irritating, humanistic understanding of those who hold power but use it sparingly. Accept the rules of the game, that's what they said. She was a pretty, easy-going woman, he discovered, and was perturbed by the idea that he was such a transparent man — he imagined that everyone could immediately see what was going through his mind. In its mother's arms, the baby moved its head and yawned, eyes closed. Could it be that, like this, no one would notice it wasn't normal? Babies, even his, were all alike. For a good while, until the child grew, he mused, they could take him out without having to provide any additional explanation.

In the next room was the doctor — a tired, humourless old man who smiled testily when he took the baby and placed it on the small table covered with a sheet and blanket. As he removed its clothes, which he did almost harshly, he spouted random information about the syndrome in a monotonous voice — and the young father noticed, feeling silent pricks in his soul, that there was a measured brutality in each word. Each word was strictly true, of that there was no doubt, but he felt as if a big lie was unfolding, whose source he was unable to locate. Maybe I'm the lie, he thought. Now he sat at the table, his eyes drawn to a book on whose cover he made out the words 'mongolism' and 'stimulation', and immediately reached for it, but the doctor beat him to it and, as if merely clearing the terrain, whisked it into a drawer. In the same instant, a pencil and paper appeared — and the man started drawing lines and jotting down numbers, as if preparing to demonstrate a theorem.

'Your baby, with enough stimulation, may attain 50, 60 per cent of the intelligence of a normal child. And, if well looked after, he may even be able to lead an almost normal life, with relative autonomy. Now let's see how his heart is.'

A kind of lesson for idiots. He placed the stethoscope in his ears and, as if deciphering a message from beyond, his eyes almost closed, a network of wrinkles on his aged face, the tribal medicine man listened to the baby's heart for a few minutes, moving the metal disc (which must have felt cold, the father imagined, his own skin rising up in goose pimples) millimetrically across its chest. The resident smiled — it's just routine, don't worry, she appeared to be saying. His wife was tense. The father waited, the 50 per cent of intelligence still thumping in his soul. Why should someone like that live? But his profound, inexplicable irritation at what he judged gruffness on the part of the doctor, present in each gesture, his grossness, the superiority of one who was merely staring at a small statistic (he no doubt had something better to be doing than repeating this idiotic ABC to ignorant parents), ended up aligning him with his son, as if presented with a challenge, which got up his nose even more because he was defeated from the start. The doctor, his eyes pressed firmly closed, turned his face to the ceiling and creased his crumpled forehead even more, his stethoscope hand receiving a message.

'He has a murmur.'

He ignored the parents — he was talking to the resident. In the steely silence that followed, she placed her stethoscope on the baby's chest and listened, a resident learning a lesson. But she was reluctant to agree.

'I don't think so.'

She kept listening, since the doctor didn't say anything in return — for him, her agreement was just a matter of time; the murmur was obvious. Another half-minute of searching.

'I can't hear it,' she said.

The baby's arms and legs moved in silence. The doctor listened again, with a brusque, challenged gesture. He took a little longer. He concentrated, eyes closed. His reputation seemed to be at stake.

'Here. Definitely. A murmur.'

The young father immediately imagined a scalpel slicing his son's chest open, looking for a defect impossible to resolve amidst so much blood, gloved fingers pulling out a tiny, useless heart, still beating — he wouldn't survive the operation. But it was as if the resident's steadfastness redeemed him.

'I don't think it's a murmur.'

The father actually had the presence of spirit to consider the beauty of the word: a murmur. Something soft, which appears and disappears. But the resident's determination to defend the baby from that phantom murmur saved his morning. There was someone on his side, it seemed. It was no longer the baby who was at stake now, but a pretty woman against a stupid ogre. Whatever she says will always be better than what he says, he thought. Maybe it was the good cop/bad cop routine. The good cop (the resident) was there to soften the blow of reality, which was the job of the bad cop, the unpleasant old doctor. There was no doubt about it: a heart problem was on its way, insisted the doctor. And she answered back, perhaps breaking their previously agreed-upon script: the baby doesn't have anything, which created an uneasy atmosphere that no longer had anything to do with his son, who finally began to cry his slow cry, while the doctors almost argued. His wife picked up the baby, now dressed, and rocked him, while he concentrated on the doctors' conversation — there was tension there. They were told to take the baby to another doctor, a super-specialist, whose only job, it seemed, was to discover things like this — whether a murmur was a murmur or something else.

'But there's no doubt,' said the old doctor, 'it's a heart condition.'

Which the young resident, smiling, answered with her eyes, while walking them back to the corridor — don't worry, it's nothing, she seemed to be saying. Back in the real world, a simple exam with another specialist confirmed that there was nothing wrong with Felipe's heart.

Write, pretend nothing was going on and write. Taking refuge in this silence, he returned to his literature, as before. In a circle of friends — his return to the tribe — he read aloud chapter four of *Essay on Passion*, which he kept writing to forget everything else. Reading aloud was something he never did again for the rest of his life, but at that moment, hearing his own voice and laughing at his own wittiness, with the exact audience, it was soothing. He wrote about other things, not his son or his life — in fact, Down syndrome did not appear in his work at any point, for over twenty years. It's your problem, he told himself, no one else's, and you'll have to solve it by yourself. He talked out loud and laughed a lot — he refused to be defeated by the shame he felt of his son, even if he had to perform mental acrobatics every time he spoke about him in public. Perhaps he could pretend his son still hadn't been born — that something was going to happen before the irremediable did. Write, he told himself — you are a writer. Do what you can — the rest will come on its own.

The baby was fine, quiet in his room. There wasn't much to be done. The father already knew that he needed to be stimulated, but the information was meagre and vague, and he hated doctors, nurses, hospitals, wards, treatments, medicines, sick people, health plans (he'd never had one), prescriptions, recommended doses, chemists. He had a hard time looking at his son — a constant reminder of all those things he didn't like. He specifically asked his lecturer friend not to publish the poem, that ridiculous poem, and apparently (he remembered vaguely) she'd said yes, the thing would be taken out of the magazine. It was a relief. The readers should be spared that awful drivel.

But 'Nothing That Wasn't' — accompanied by the image of his brother presenting him with that pseudo-philosophy in verse that he himself had written as an antidote to the horror of life — sprung to mind from time to time, and it irritated him every time. The poem argued in defence of an optimistic fatalism: things happen inevitably and are already in writing somewhere, thus indisputable. The simple fact that they happen is already something to be respected: the simple, brutal weight of reality, that which you can touch with your hand. It took his son being born to make him see, suddenly, the ugly crack in the cosmic optimism he'd borrowed from somewhere as an aesthetic frame for his own life: so beautiful, everything is in everything, present time contained in past time, celestial harmony — and us, cardboard creatures, participating in the spectacle of the universe as guests of honour. Wise up: accept it.

But he formulated a reaction, or at least managed to verbalise what had really oriented his life to that point: I am not condemned to anything — I refuse to condemn myself to anything, no matter what. I've always managed to change direction, when I had to. It was a kind of bravado, he knew it — but he had to start somewhere. Where? Right where I am, here, now, today, me and my mentally handicapped child, for all time. This child, in this moment, he figured, is absolutely nothing. It is an organic being trying to survive, and nothing else. In this he is the same as any other child, normal or abnormal, anyplace, anywhere in the world. Here and now: if he'd died at two days of age from the non-existent heart problem, if he'd suddenly been struck down by some other kind of mutation at four days of age or for any other random reason out of all those possible, well — there we'd be at dusk in the cemetery, under the shade of that beautiful tree, receiving condolences, with a sigh of relief. It's better this way, everyone would whisper. Their friends' tight hugs — how good they'd be! His son wouldn't have had time to receive from others any living contour beyond the world of reflexes and his own name at the registry office. He wouldn't have been anything beyond biological life — a still-strange being, to whom we, his parents, have given the gift of a presence, and nothing else. The idea of a child: that is what I need, he might have said if he'd managed to articulate what he felt more clearly. This child gives me no future, he found himself saying. I'm not condemned to anything, he almost said aloud. I can go to Mozambique to teach Portuguese to a lost tribe, and never return. Or get into the United States and work as a sweeper (I did it in Germany and I can do it again) while writing books that will make me famous, under another name. I can — he found himself saying, with growing irritation at his own impotence. He opened another beer, and was thinking vaguely that he needed to eat something, when the phone rang.

He suddenly remembered that something was still missing for it to be irremediable: the genetic confirmation — one last, improbable card up his sleeve, a fleeting illusion of salvation, a chromosomal miracle. The answer was at the other end of the line. He held his breath. But his last crutch collapsed.

'It's confirmed. The karyotype says it really is trisomy 21.'

Both father and mother fell silent. They had to wait for the stone to slowly settle at the bottom of the lake, sinking further and further into the wet sand, in the scum and gloom. They had to feel the consistency of the weight that would remain with them for the rest of time, heavy in their souls, before saying anything. Bucking, stubborn monosyllables — they couldn't look at one another.

'We knew it.'

'We did.'

Years later, he would think: we lived in such a profoundly abstract way that the child's presence and all its evidence wasn't enough for it to really be something. We needed an official document, a paper, a stamp, proof of something unknowable, an illegible photograph, those little black lines dancing against the chaos of a grey backdrop, now ordered according to size and type, one by one, in two columns, giving scientific order to the chaos of real life, to determine the nature of a life. Not the chromosome — which was irrelevant because it was incomprehensible — but the photograph of the chromosome, already reorganised to provide us with its meaning and explanation.

Three strangers in silence. There was nothing to embrace.

Once the diagnosis was confirmed, they needed an assessment by specialists, in order to prepare for the early stimulation of their child that was supposed to start as soon as possible. To protect himself from the glum perspective of the insane work that he, in darkness, imagined useless, he repeated the cliché, 'Life is an obstacle course,' smiling. It gave him a kind of emotional respite: the joke and the smile. Obstacles: the word was alive. Spoken aloud, it was a stone rolling over in his mouth. Obstacles, obstacles, he repeated, to see if it kept its strength.

He now held a book in his hands, an object more powerful than real life — capable of explaining it, formatting it, drawing it, subverting it and even substituting it, sometimes with advantages. A family guidebook for parents with mongoloid children. On the blue cover was the word 'mongolism' — slightly less offensive. And the author, an absolute expert on the subject, had science behind him. The power of science was respectable. Another path to salvation opened up to him — it didn't take much to enthuse him; with that child in his arms, the world began again every morning, and anything was better than nothing when you had a non-child on your hands. It was his wife, however, who had found the book and brought it to him. A few phone calls and they jotted down the address — they were going to São Paulo for an assessment. Fantasy immediately swamped his head again, an irrational daydream that, nonetheless, calmed him — the doctor was going to be completely taken aback by the boy's potential. Flicking through the book, he jotted down the reference to Jean Piaget, and bought *The Origin of Intelligence in Children* so he could read straight from the source and do the tests himself. (It was a way, he would think many years later, of anticipating and freeing himself of the diagnosis by the authority on the subject. He didn't want to stay in his designated place, that of an obedient father, or worse, of an apprentice father. He would never lose his arrogant nature.)

He was still bucking; he still hadn't left the maternity ward; he still hadn't taken the child home. He still hadn't begun to live — this web arresting his gestures, this uncertain future, this silent child in his arms. Intelligence is the only important value in life; there's nothing else. It's the only thing that determines my degree of humanity, he mused, going to great lengths to avoid saying things exactly like that, in that explicit anti-Christianity. He just felt that that was how things were, and pretended not to accept them, but he was unable to rid himself of the rule and ruler. They shoot horses, don't they? He remembered the book by Horace McCoy, looking for comparisons, which was ridiculous. Blaming the desire for exclusion on mercy. Yes, they do kill horses, don't they, he repeated, to feel the extent of the truth. But the moral counterweight was so overwhelming that the mere idea faded away. The ability to forget and start over: that was his core quality, he thought. He still didn't realise it, but he was beginning to have an idea of a child, to create a hypothesis for it. As if, still very timidly, paternity was finally beginning to cast its shadow over him.

And he started here, too, to set the trap from which it

would be so hard to free himself. The problem wasn't his son; the problem was him. If the problem was his son, he, the father, would have been lost, but he didn't know this yet. He was about to start the race according to other people's rules — in fact, truth be told, according to the rules he had accepted. The idea of transformation still hadn't occurred to him — all he could do was condemn the essence of the problem. He still thought he was the same person, day after day; it was as if he were dragging around his own ghost, which was getting heavier and heavier, month after month. Better to leave it behind, leave himself behind, peel away from himself like a special effect and start over, light as a feather. But what to do with his son in this liberating transformation? His son was heavy; he had to be dragged along. Or, at least, he had to work out who the intruder was.

São Paulo was a city he liked a lot — an abstract combination of infinite lines and forms organising the entire world into squares, and making it such a brutally human creation that there wasn't the slightest crack for nature to get through. A world of moving heads that inhabited a map, not a space. They were moving ideas and projects, not people. He felt at home, although in the deepest layer of memory he could hear his childhood guru cursing megalopolises as the climax of anti-humanism and the final defeat of the good savage. The Tietê River was rotting, while buildings rose up to the sky; the asphalt that separated us from nature was also humankind in its essence. Or, he thought, smiling, would I prefer to cut up tobacco while squatting on my haunches or sitting on a three-legged stool to keep my balance? The moderate would say that progress and nature were not incompatible, but some civilisation was necessary between one thing and another, and in Brazil it seemed there was no time for anything — between one project and another, there was a sea of people who got crushed along the way. The country couldn't provide for everyone, but what could you do? Such a big nation! What could you do?

Down the busy Paulista Avenue he went, his little problem in his arms, accompanied by his wife, carrying the bag of paraphernalia required for a baby's survival. The baby, insidiously, was almost no trouble whatsoever. Mongoloid children sleep a lot, are hypotonic, slow at everything. Like the witch's test in 'Hansel and Gretel', every day he rubbed his index finger in the baby's palm, which immediately clamped around it, squeezing it, in a reflex that seemed normal. Maybe he doesn't have anything wrong with him, he thought. We won't have to put him in the oven. He laughed, lacking the courage to share his black humour with his wife.

The doctor's office gave him back his sense of the harshest reality. There he was, surrounded by the wealthy, the crème de la crème, tasteful pictures on the walls, clean upholstery, air-conditioning, a polite, efficient receptionist, the consultation paid for and scheduled, which, of course, would be the only flaw. Like a mysterious kind of contradiction to confirm absolute authority, an offensive lack of punctuality was a universal rule of the profession, a kind of code to distance its members from the smallest, most mundane, human condition. He'd never seen anyone complain to a doctor about their lack of punctuality; at the most, a polite question to the receptionist, more of a worried 'Excuse me', just out of curiosity, hands behind their back, head down, than an actual complaint. He grew irritated with himself, with the fact that he was looking for a reason to get irritated, and this put him back with the herd again, the cattle, bucking against the fence. His wife, on the other hand, looked calm. The baby, as always, was also calm. If he complained to the receptionist about the doctor's non-punctuality, she'd immediately give him a reasonable explanation for the delay (an emergency call-out, a consultation slotted in at the last minute, a traffic jam), which, before even hearing the explanation, piqued his irritation — the fact that doctors, a bunch he despised, were always right. Maybe his irritation was due to the alcohol. They were staying in an enormous flat that belonged to some distant but very kind friends, and the night before he'd stayed up late talking with one of them, a young alcoholic, and he'd drunk more than he should have. In the end, at the crack of dawn, as he got up crooked from the armchair to go to bed (he remembered this now, and the memory was like an electric shock — how could he have forgotten?), the young alcoholic, who would never finish high school, had slurred, 'You're so intelligent, but you couldn't even make a kid properly.' He heard laughter, still echoing.

He walked into the doctor's office with that echo in his head, trying to understand what he had heard through to his innermost layer, but there were so many superimposed layers now that he was facing the doctor and her assistant. They were polite and cold, and as he handed over the baby he felt deeply that he had already been defeated. Here, there was a real ruler to measure him with. Science was made of tables and recurrent signs, of course — otherwise we'd be back in the Middle Ages, trusting mysterious signs that could only be decoded by witches, without compassion. There was no compassion here either, but a presupposition of reality, finally separate from God, the hypothesis of whose existence didn't count, or we'd be back in the kingdom of chance and arbitrariness, in the hands of high priests and their own designs. Not here: icy science was his guarantee. And with each preliminary measurement, his son was reduced to himself, to his implacable biological form, to the limits of his

DNA, to the short reach of the powers of his code. What am I doing here? It's me who needs analysis, not the baby.

They learned nothing new, of course. The diagnosis was what he already knew before the baby was examined. And because the baby still wasn't anyone, sleepy and indifferent to the hell around him, the doctor addressed herself to the parents, repeating everything they already knew. Science doesn't have or make miracles. They listened to a sermon on the advantages of early stimulation and some sundry advice. The book was self-explanatory. There were psychological issues involved that, if given the right attention, could alleviate the burden of the child. His wife listened to each word with great attention, while he daydreamed, trying to find, between the cracks in that serious, severe speech that was being delivered from the height of authority, something truly useful. But he was unable to. The doctor didn't see anything particularly noteworthy in the child, no special quality that caught her attention. She didn't smile. She was an impersonal spokesperson for science, and had the obligation to say things exactly as they were — and things weren't good, because they weren't normal and they fell outside every standard measurement in every aspect: a trisomy of chromosome 21 was aggressively present in every cell of the baby's body. That was it. Off you go with your little bundle, she seemed to be saying, when she finally smiled her professional smile. Say things as they are: don't complain, he found himself thinking. You want to hear a lie, but the doctor doesn't have one to give you. You want a secret gesture of mercy, disguised by the hand of science, but there's a shortage of that, too. For centuries, life's functions have all been separated, each in its specialty. What she has to say, in addition to scientifically describing the syndrome, is what you can do for the child, but don't get your hopes up; at the most, you will make things bearable. You are not the only one, nor will you be the last.

Outside, he finally lit a cigarette and took a deep, tasty puff, gazing up at the funnel of buildings against the blue sky.

Two weeks later, a newspaper clipping found its way into his hands — a clinic in Rio de Janeiro was offering a full early-stimulation program for children with Down syndrome (the article had used the word 'mongolism' in brackets), applying techniques traditionally used for brain-damage sufferers, something completely different. 'A full program' — after his insipid experience with the doctor in São Paulo, the idea pleased him. He'd always liked full courses: things had to have a beginning, a middle, and an end, like life, and preferably in that order. Nothing by halves, and (as he lit a cigarette, rereading the short article for the thirtieth time) he thought about his son as a half. Difficult days: the baby still hadn't learned to suckle properly, and they had to continue the engineering with the medieval glass cornet to extract from his wife's breasts, in the most primitive way, that liquid of undefined colour, which they ended up mixing with a particular brand of tinned milk, the only one the baby would take.

The first child of any marriage is a monumental hassle. The intruder required space and attention: cried too much, had no fixed hours or limits, and practically no language in common; couldn't control anything about his body, which was always bubbling away of its own accord; depended on a enormous array of objects hitherto unknown to them (cradles, bottles, plastic funnels, and nappies — thousands of them); was a drain on their finances, time, patience, and tolerance; suffered inexplicable, untranslatable ills; established a fear of fragility and ignorance around itself; and came between his parents, almost as if he were kicking them apart. And he was ugly, like all newborns. It was hard to imagine that time alone could make a human being spring from that crumpled thing, as if by magic. In his case, he thought (lighting another cigarette), for nothing. Calling a spade a spade, he concluded daily: this child would give him nothing in return — not even that petty, but reasonable pleasure of showing him to others like a trophy, already divining secret and unprecedented qualities in the future of that (which would one day be a) beautiful being. If I write a book about him, or for him, he thought, he'll never be able to read it.

A full program. He turned the article over in his hand, while his wife, who had discovered it, waited for a verdict. She was the one who always decided everything, but there was still a sexist ritual to perform: they had both been born in 1952, and for a long time paid the price of their era — he more so than she. The overwhelming majority of men were emotionally retarded, he joked, which was a good excuse to stay put. In those first few days (hard, harrowing, incomplete, silent), his mother-in-law helped a lot, which relieved him. The doctor who'd taught that class to soon-to-be parents was right, he had to admit. He wanted as much distance from the baby as possible. In the morning he attended boring language and literature classes at the university, and felt the stupidity of his own aggressiveness, which he was almost always able to contain. He needed the degree to survive — one day he was going to make a living from what he did, he hoped. In the afternoon he'd write one or two pages, inching forward in his book like someone escaping from the world through a secret passage. At night he'd go out — he went to taverns to drink beer and chat, but almost never about his son. Whenever anyone asked, he answered 'Fine' and gave them a disarming smile, followed by a counter-question to change the topic. The world was elsewhere, not with him.

Walking through the city one sudden morning, he felt the strangeness of his footsteps, resounding in absurd silence amidst a crowd of strangers. He was struck once again by the hard, unshakable notion that he was no longer the same person, that he had now permanently crossed over to another side, still unknown, from which there was absolutely no return, and that he was condemned to be a slave to a never-ending present in which he was not proficient.

It was a familiar downtown street. Years earlier, he remembered, he'd walked down that same street late at night with two or three friends, taking swigs from a bottle. It was such an innocent world: right in the middle of the financial district they'd unscrewed a huge glass sign from a wall and hauled it along for blocks and blocks, as if carrying furniture, until they finally smashed it in the middle of the asphalt, tossing it up with a primal war cry. The splintering glass reverberated in his woozy head, and the dim lights came alive in a supernatural echo. Curitiba was a ghost town, and he, at the age of fifteen, had believed he was in charge of his own actions.

On another unforgettable night, he smashed a bookstore window with a small iron bar. He and his friend, on a bench in Generoso Marques Square, examined the booty: twenty-two books, some repeated. The bad luck was that they were non-fiction. He only took two home, because he'd have to explain them if anyone asked, and he was a poor liar out loud. But he read the books to justify the crime. One was on the evils of the American Empire, with an aggressive eagle on the cover. Another, on the advantages of the world of socialism, with the title in red. Two days later, the robbery got a brief mention in the newspaper, and he bragged about his feat to his actor friend at school, proudly showing him the clipping.

Tetrachloroethylene, he remembered, like a charm — he had made a pinprick in some capsules of the substance, emptied them into a handkerchief, and sniffed it. He had bought the worm medicine at a chemist's, taking the name on a piece of paper to give his request credibility. It was perhaps the only transcendence of his life, a kind of physical transportation to nowhere at all, a tiny sensorial roller coaster. I got out of that one, he remembered now, but not exactly with relief. All that's left is the ground I'm standing on, this exact spot, not a smidgen more. It's like collapsing, not waking up. No one wakes up, he thought, crossing Osório Square that sunny morning. We just collapse. He felt again an emptiness that he wanted to fill with something very close to the eyes and the soul, and which would be like a key, finally opening a tricky door. He slowed down, ignored a begging boy, and stepped up onto the pavement. Perhaps, he thought (now overcome with a feeling of no return, his useless memory throwing up images from years and years before, as if they were saying something, or had something urgent to say, some secret meaning seeking to be deciphered, but they didn't, they were just small ghosts of time, fragments of nothing, and finally, it seemed, he was on the other side now, as if he'd absorbed the inevitable, without resistance), there is no return. Now it's up to you. He felt a ridiculous spasm in his throat, his body demanding tears and he denying himself the right. He stopped in his tracks. The shame, the day, was too bright — someone noticed he was crying, and it hurt. He did an about-turn, took another street, and another, but they all led nowhere.

In 1981, Rio de Janeiro was as beautiful as always. Once again, he felt the impact of the enormous spaces opening to the sea and the delicacy of the city's silhouettes against the blue sky — a memory of his time as an almost–naval officer. Before going to the clinic, he took a taxi with his wife and three-month-old son to the neighbourhood of Urca to visit one of his high school friends, who was now a theatre and TV actor in Rio. His friend's boyfriend, practically a child, answered the door politely. He felt another strangeness, one world on top of another, in layers. It startled him, as if he was already definitively from another time. Everyone (he thought, gazing at the sea on the beautiful ride back, the baby in his lap) is at the limit, permanently at the limit of themselves; yet all there is on the other side is time. All it took was one step forward. He closed his eyes and took refuge in time: nothing that isn't could have been, and again he felt irritated. This can't be all there is. But it's a good excuse, a kind of breather. Relax; time is slipping past. Time can't do anything to hurt you, he thought, besides age you, and at this stage that's a good thing. 'Age!' writer Nelson Rodrigues had advised young people, and he smiled as he remembered.

In January 1972 he and his friend had participated in a theatre festival in the city of Caruaru, in Brazil's north-east, and they'd hitched back, rucksacks on their backs, thumbing lifts, crossing Brazil on foot. In Salvador, they'd slept out in the open, on the sands of the mythical Itapuã Beach. On the outskirts of town, as they passed a long stretch of road works on the hard shoulder of the highway, looking for what looked like a good place to wait, a petrol station a little further along, workmen intrigued by the two long-haired characters — poorly dressed, like themselves, but in a different way — asked what they did. 'Theatre,' answered his friend. 'What's theatre?' one of them asked, sincerely curious. 'It's a kind of circus,' he'd answered, after stuttering a little, confused. He felt bad — a harsh strangeness between two worlds. How can someone not know what theatre is? he asked himself, stupidly.

At another moment in their long journey, they'd spent their last few pennies buying a hunk of white cheese on the roadside, which had to last them a good while. A short time later, as it was growing dark, they got a lift in the empty wagon of a truck that was going as far as Macaé, in the state of Rio de Janeiro. Further along, late at night, the truck stopped again, and an entire family of migrants from the north-east started piling on. It seemed endless: a man, his wife, an uncle, an aunt, the grandfather, a saki monkey on a child's shoulder, another child, a girl, two cousins, a baby, another man, some tools, hoes and scythes, another woman, pregnant, a skinny dog on a frayed collar, tattered bags, and another old woman. Everyone in that truck, human and animal, stank, and the two actors kept moving back until they found themselves with their backs to the cabin, barely managing to hide the cheese. The physical proximity was disconcerting. The migrants seemed to be staring at them in the dark, the night suddenly illuminated by a postcard full moon, perfect for a Portinari-style panel that looked as fake as a cardboard cut-out against a painted sky. He contemplated the live wind-whipped etching. The migrants barely spoke. They whispered to one another from time to time, hanging on as best they could as the truck barrelled along. When it was finally time to eat their cheese, he and his friend offered to share it only as a gesture of politeness — but in the same instant a penknife appeared out of somewhere, and the pieces were cut and distributed in religious silence, with the thankful reverence of those receiving communion. It occurred to him that he'd like to know what time it was, but he was ashamed to take out his pocket-watch, attached to the waistband of his threadbare pants with a silver chain, the would-be writer's dandy touch.

The clinic was on a hill, surrounded by greenery. Years later, he would vividly remember that building with its blue lines, imposing like an old school, and the anxiety with which he approached it — his permanent anxiety when faced with new situations and the dangers of losing, or even scratching, his self-esteem. Perhaps that was it, he thought, fighting the idea. Perhaps it was that his son had broken his back, which he'd gone to such lengths to hold upright. It was a chance happening. Everything could have been different, but time was unredeemable. Chance and non-chance brought me here, he thought, as he waited to be seen. Chance is in my wife's arms; we, who were once chance, are here by choice. A full program, he remembered, that could keep them busy. There he was again in the waiting rooms of hospitals, of clinics, of wards, of the shadows of illnesses and death, of sterile corridors. His back was broken, he thought again. Poverty was all around him: handicaps were a thing of the poor, the bedraggled, the miserable, migrants, the needy — their knitted brows demanding some kind of justice, their eyes lowering just before the club came smashing down on their heads. Beggars grovelled on street corners — echoes of an immortal, squatting poverty, the shame of being alive reverberating through the centuries. Nevertheless, here I am, with my little leper in my arms, to the delight of some imaginary mother superior arriving in the hospital atrium in her only moment of true happiness, after a lifetime of self-inflicted punishment, the scourge of the soul, but she needs to take someone with her to her own private hell fire — and the mother superior smiled, all dressed in black in her small day-to-day death, a fake smile, her fingernails reaching forward to stroke the unsuspecting baby's head as he slept.

He shook his head. I'm going crazy. The name for this is resentment, he thought. The young woman who greeted them was kind and determined. Don't be quick to judge, he told himself. She repeated an old cliché, which he barely heard: the parents aren't the problem; they're the solution. He wished he wasn't there. He wished he was at home, smoking a cigarette and writing his book, which talked about other, much more important things than this pragmatism which, no matter where he looked, got tangled not in sentiments of humanity but in religion — our small, clingy, day-to-day transcendence. It was a group program. After an individual evaluation, they'd have a full itinerary, a lesson, a system, a chart to follow. They climbed a flight of stairs and walked down a corridor. It's definitely a thing of the poor, because there are infinitely more poor people in the world than rich people — he returned to his train of thought — and therefore everything that is poor is overtly conspicuous; it is everywhere with its hand out. It isn't a curse; it's pure statistics. Entire governments are made by these outstretched hands out alone.

Another few steps, and he stopped in front of an open door leading into a room, where he saw the most unforgettable sight of his life. He was unable to contain his shock: somewhere in the deepest layer of his soul he was certain that this would be his world, and no other, until the end of time. There were dozens of people, children, teenagers, adults, all irremediably handicapped, in a courtyard of miraculous deformities — arms that didn't obey commands, mouths that opened but didn't shut, ineffectual eyes, the rictus of exasperating desires that gestures could not fulfil, splayed fingers, always halfway there; and there was, in everything, a kind of shadow of a dual universe crushed by an insurmountable present. They were nowhere at all. Space was the floor; time, an inaccessible luxury. And what were they doing? They were all crawling about on the floor — but here the crawling was, in practice, the true path to cure, the first exercise designed to give the handicapped back power (or some of it) over their own flesh. But that wasn't all: their bodies were placed on the ground so they could rediscover the design of their nervous systems and recover something of what had been lost. The delirium of a utopia: rediscovering the kernel of the species that had clambered out of the water to drag itself across dry land. The human spinal cord conserved this memory, they said, and it needed to be reawakened. It was Plato's cave in the kingdom of neurology.

There was a crude touch that made the scene even more Dantesque. They were all wearing rudimentary plastic masks on their faces that covered their noses and mouths to such an extent that they had a hard time breathing, and that was precisely the idea. With oxygen momentarily scarce, their lungs tried harder, making a super-human effort to recover what they were missing — air — and their hands finally managed to reach the mask to tear it off. The renewed air brutally oxygenised their brains in a double dose, but not for long. The mask was put back on them for another sequence. It was simple: create problems so they'd have to save themselves. He couldn't tear his eyes away from that purgatory in which absolutely nothing fitted the norm, in which every movement disobeyed the intent behind it — a kind of collective absence, a parallel world, where all concerned (injured, handicapped, or trisomic) were placed side by side in the same endless race to nowhere. He still hadn't the faintest idea of the differences between them: the whole thing was the difference. The brutality of it. War might be worse, he thought, tumbling from the heights of his delicateness, his foot in the door of that crooked — yes, really crooked — world. They were crooked angels, who were born, lived, and died in the shadows.

And then, finally, he looked up from the ground, and there were the women (just women) who made that machine function. There were mothers, aunts, grandmothers, and maids, he figured, running his eyes across their faces, who'd brought their disabled for their physiotherapy sessions. Their faces were at once patient and tense. He recognised, for the first time, the syndrome of parents with disabled children: their faces were marked with a subcutaneous layer of tension, a sharp gaze, worried and incomplete, always with the shadow of a justification on the tip of their tongues, which sometimes (in the beginning) spilled over into despair but was quickly brought under control, because civilisation was powerful. We can't grab hold of people and shake them to make them look at us. Later, little by little, he acquired the discreet awareness of one who was definitively on the outside of life, where the rest was just a matter of practical details — the world was only ten metres in diameter. This is where we move, he thought.

The woman gently pulled him back from the door. 'Let's go. It's at the end of the corridor.'

He prised his eyes away from the room with some effort, and they went with the woman to do the evaluation. This is all too familiar, he thought — except for the scene in the room. He still hadn't woken up from it — the impact of reality, the aesthetic of horror. Could it be normalised? That is, could unexpected people be a part of normal life? He was far too delicate, or ignorant, or stupid, or irremediably immature to face up to simple reality. His first thought was petty: my son's case is different. He isn't brain-damaged — he has a genetic syndrome. He won't need to writhe about on the floor to learn to move his arms. There was also an aesthetic criterion in this advantage: trisomic children looked like tiny adults, miniature humans, circus dwarves. They weren't as harsh on the eyes as crippled children were. With the right work, they could be absorbed into the system, he imagined. But what work? Making them as much like human beings as possible — that would make everyone happy. This tiny rung of superiority was his brief refuge when he walked into the room for the first evaluation. They asked questions, filled in a form, examined the child — weight, size, reflexes, characteristics. The usual. But there was an atmosphere of almost frenetic activity, which was contagious. It was a collective undertaking, and he felt a cheer in the air, an almost visible optimism, and saw empathy on their faces. For the first time, he felt his son was an individual, which surprised him, as if they were lying. But the instruction wasn't individual — the clinic saw groups of people interested in the program on specific dates. The price was high, but there appeared to be subsidies for the poor — all one had to do was look around.

First there were forms to be filled in, case by case, then everyone listened to lectures; finally, treatment programs were drawn up according to individual needs. Yes, a full program: somewhere in his watchmaker's head a seed of salvation had been planted. It still wasn't the image of his son, who was finally starting to become someone in his life, someone with whom he interacted; it was just the playful idea of a game, an ingenious mechanism of stimuli in which, if played well, a problem-child placed at this end of the tunnel would emerge at the other like any other child. He still avoided the word 'normal', but it was the idea that fuelled the clinic. He didn't know it yet, but he was already completely on board — like a grown-up kid receiving a perpetuum mobile kit and obsessing about assembling it to perfection. There still wasn't a son in his life; just a problem to be solved, and now he'd been given a very interesting map, almost an instruction manual. Behind this little miracle, a subtle detail he hadn't considered before was beginning to appear: motivation.

His head still resisted, tugging him back here and there. This is pure behaviourism, he whispered to his wife in the first lecture. By definition, it was the branch of science in which behaviour could be explained as conditioned motor or glandular responses — a theory that had more recently fallen into the dead-end box of positivism. Basically, it was an understanding of life purely as a set of reflexes permeating all aspects of human activity, from the reading of a text to the pain one feels upon stubbing a toe. Humans were machines programmed to react, in which the world of culture could not be distinguished from the world of nature. There was a doctrinal simplicity to the lectures — the idea of 'doctrine' was more or less palpable. The clinic, it seemed, was waging a war, and saw itself as 'revolutionary'. He liked that: it seemed that at every stage of his life, from his adolescent rebellion against the 'system' to his experience with the theatre group, and the legal and illegal political notions spilling over from Brazil's long, bureaucratic military dictatorship, there had been pockets of revolutionary redemption: random, contradictory utopias here and there that contributed to a definitively better world. It was contagious. As was the impact of hearing a talk by the director of the clinic himself — a huge man in a wheelchair that he manoeuvred quickly and energetically, his arms oddly muscular and callused (he must have gone through the group crawling sessions, year after year, thought the father), his voice thunderous, somewhat tense, with an almost harsh, humourless authority — which made the father whisper to his wife, as if seeking relief from the tension, 'I think I'm going to write a short story: "The Incredible Doctor Strangelove and His Exceptional Children".' The man's authority, however, was considerable: he was himself a successful product of the method he was preaching, like the stage magician who offers to be sawn in half. A quadriplegic, he controlled his wheelchair with his iron voice and a few fingers, which, with great effort, responded to his neurological commands by pressing buttons. At one stage in his talk, he made it clear that the clinic's work was the target of criticism and subject to doctrinal tensions. 'They accuse us of creating little monkeys with conditioned reflexes. If that really is the case, why not?' What other option is there?' Yes, thought the father, we all want polite, well-behaved children who are not hard on the eyes or the soul. Children who don't provoke suspicious glances at the parents, who are ultimately responsible for the erroneous creatures. Initially mistrusting, as always (there was something he suspected was 'unscientific' in the air — something forced, a discreet falsification of reality, but it was convincing, nonetheless), he was slowly drawn into the details of the program. It would always be better than nothing, or at least much better than the random, erratic stimuli that people had told him about early on: no one had seemed to know what to do. Here, they were sure. This was momentarily reassuring for those listening.

The clinic's point of departure, the father tried to understand, was the belief that a treatment originally designed for brain-damaged patients could be perfectly applied to cases of trisomy 21 — mongolism. Some time later, opening one of the books sold by the clinic, he read the absurd assertion that the main cause of mongolism was pre-natal brain damage, caused mostly by malnutrition; the book argued that the chromosomal abnormality was the result of this brain damage, and not the other way around. Reality had to be adapted to theory at any cost. The people at the clinic, however, didn't repeat this nonsense, nor did they emphasise anything theoretical — they repeatedly stressed the importance of the parents ('They're the solution, not the problem'), and offered some mechanistic slogans that seemed inoffensive at the time, like 'the function determines the structure' — which, if it were true, would indicate a kind of triumph of Lamarck over Darwin. It didn't matter. A full program: with the enthusiasm of a tourist holding a travel brochure, he leafed through the mimeographed pages showing the daily (hourly, to be more precise) sequence of exercises with which they would occupy themselves for the next few years. They went from room to room, listening to talks and watching demonstrations. He began to feel better. In fact, the idea of normality was starting to wash over him. It's a race, he thought prosaically, diving head-first into the cliché in which he found himself: it's a race and we got off to a bad start, but with some solid work the kid will catch up with the others.

He was mostly interested in what they called 'neurological organisation' — the exercise of making arms, legs, and heads repeat the standard movements of human neurological normality. He drifted off from what he was watching, and imagined it all as the construction of the human being — a mechanical but efficient construction. Truth was, he'd succumbed to the dream. Maybe they were right, and man, in a pure state, was a machine — life had to be cleansed of its vicissitudes and useless accessories to arrive at that essence, at that imaginary waterless swimming that was being demonstrated on a table in front of him. Someone was moving a baby's head rhythmically from one side to the other, while on each side nurses moved its arms and legs in the natural cross-pattern of a human being walking. It's a production line, he thought, vaguely remembering Aldous Huxley's *Brave New World*, where this problem wouldn't exist because the genetic organisation of the world and of living things would eliminate random imperfections. According to the clinic, the child's condition (whether genetic or as the result of brain damage) affected this innate pattern of opposing arm and leg movements, and as a result the rest of the body couldn't function well. If we reinforce this point of origin (the first newts leaving the sea for land, millions of years ago, he mused, as he listened to the talk) we also work on all of the other problems — actually, we retrieve something lost. Maybe it was crazy, but it was a method. No matter how absurd it seemed (or useless, as people would sometimes tell him years later), it was always a way for him to have physical contact with his son, for his son to become a sensorial and emotional extension of himself, and to create by osmosis a complicity that he had initially thought impossible, still bucking to get out of his mental cage.

He drifted off, creating a syndrome of his own that would become more and more intense as the years went by — a growing inability to concentrate on anyone talking at length. People should speak in writing, he thought. Only six years earlier, he had been at the University of Coimbra Library, in Portugal, reading *The Rebel*, by Camus, and *The Birth of Tragedy*, by Nietzsche. He tried to calculate what month that had been, staring at the ceiling and fluorescent lights: yes, it was the same time of year. My formative years, he thought, quickly anticipating his own old age. He felt as if he was always lagging behind. If he'd had the gift of cold analysis, he'd have said he still hadn't been born then. One year in Europe, with very little money and lots of books. He remembered how he used to go into supermarkets wearing a huge coat, and come out with his pockets stuffed with tins of tuna and sardines, which he stocked in his cupboard in the pension. All he had to do was buy some bread, and he was fed. A crook: he had a legitimate occupation as a crook, and he gave an imaginary chuckle, as if explaining his thieving technique to a group of friends amidst beers and laughter.

Maybe if he were doing this now he'd have a political explanation up his sleeve: a military dictatorship was, itself, the demise of law — and the 1970s had been universally seen as a time when respect for the law collapsed. Let's take shortcuts, everyone both on the left and the right used to say. Before that, it had been a free-for-all because God didn't exist; now that God was no longer in the picture, it was a free-for-all because the state itself was criminal. While he daydreamed, the mothers and fathers around him listened attentively to the talk on opposing arms and legs, and neurological maturing. In 1975, he'd slept during the day and kept the night, well into the wee hours, until dawn, for reading and writing, in his Raskolnikov's attic, where, if he stood suddenly, he'd hit his head on the roof beam. The street was called Rua Afonso Henriques, he remembered, in Upper Coimbra. There he wrote his defining poem, with Rousseau and Marx in his head, Freud more or less useless in his vest pocket, and paradise on the horizon: *All forces are united so the new day will dawn.*

He'd gone out once with a friend from the Communist Party to paint scythes and hammers on the city's lampposts, just as they might have gone to play snooker, drink wine, or toss stones into the waters of the Mondego while talking about literature into the small hours. He was good at it, at the painting, he remembered. The scythe and hammer came perfectly out of two quick brush strokes — Portugal was about to burn, he daydreamed. With one interim government after another, it seemed as if they were one step away from the Final Revolution: paradise instated. (What would he be? The first dissident? The first to be shot by a firing squad? The doorman of some gulag? Our Man on the Student Council? Or, most likely, an anonymous, frightened soul trying to survive in the shadows?) They'd listened to speeches at the party headquarters in Coimbra. The legendary communist leader Álvaro Cunhal released his drawings from prison — realist quill-pen drawings whose copies were sold to raise funds for the grand cause. There was a certain feeling of 1917 in the air, of *To the Finland Station.* In one text, Cunhal explained that passports for the Russians were like ID cards for the Portuguese, which was why one had to show their passport to get from one side of the Soviet Union to the other, but in Portugal the fascist right wanted them to believe that people in Russia didn't have the right to come and go freely. They shall not pass!

He remembered participating in a march of red flags through Coimbra's narrow medieval streets. Yes, the Middle Ages were still alive in Portugal. The Portuguese were the only people with a Romance language to accept the papal order to change the names of weekdays from Roman pagan nomenclature to the tedious, ecclesiastical numbered system: 'first day', 'second day'...* They were an obedient people, capable of changing by simple decree the names of their own days. And there he was, carrying a ridiculous flag, an accidental communist, like Chaplin turning a corner. He left before the end, without hearing all of the speeches that thundered out of a military-barracks window, and handed his flag to someone else. They should pay the revolutionary workers something, he lamented. He wandered through the city centre and found an amazing bookshop — a dark, irregular cave with piles of books everywhere he looked, a space for bibliophiles, bookworms, lovers of literature. Deep in a corner of that maze, glancing around in a cold sweat, he stuffed a beautiful Penguin edition of short stories by Hemingway into his coat pocket. After all, like him (and he felt a pang of emotion, a feeling that he was somehow actively participating in human history), Hemingway had also been a revolutionary tourist, opposed to the same Franco who, like Tolkien's immortal mythical villains, was still agonising on his deathbed, rosary in hand, in the country next door — Spain's leader by the grace of God.

Why, exactly, was he remembering it all so clearly right

* Literally 'second-fair', 'third-fair', etc, the 'fair' being derived from the Latin *feria*, meaning 'celebration'.

now? The doctor was explaining the stages of neurological development, and there was a colourful, attractive picture on the wall detailing it all — bulbospinal development (grasping and light reflexes ...), the pons (commando crawling, crying response, perception of contour ...), the midbrain (voluntary grasping ...), and the cerebral cortex (cortical opposition in one hand ...). He almost gave in to self-pity, imagining a scenario in which he, a good lad, who, when he'd finally managed to get his life on track (wife, salary, regular studies, a future, books, etc.), had been given a wrong child by God — not to save him, but to enslave him, which was his lot. It was like yet another of those awful Old Testament tests, in which a sadistic God sucked his victim's souls dry, so he definitely wouldn't make anything of himself, just a shadow in the shadow of a higher power. Why? No reason, just because we will return to dust. He sighed. It would be nice if it were that simple: an explanation would do. The problem is precisely the opposite, he thought. There is no explanation. You're here because of an erratic sum of chances and choices, he told himself. God doesn't even remotely come into it. Nothing leads necessarily to anything, you're always buried alive in the present, and the presence of time — this absurd voracity — is unredeemable, as T. S. Eliot would have said. Deal with it. It's your turn.

There was complete silence around him.

It was his own reflexes that were conditioned — whenever the father remembered, he held out his finger for his son to grasp, without thinking. Neither of us thinks, he mused, placing him on the living-room floor and staring at him. The baby seemed to feel the weight of his own head, trying to hold it up and keep it steady. It wasn't easy. He had to leave him there; if he managed to roll over for some well-deserved rest, gazing at the ceiling, he had to be rolled back, and the battle to hold up his head began again. Measured cruelty, it seemed. But no; the baby didn't complain. Facing down again, he lifted his head and moved his arms as if merely beginning his work.

He still wasn't exactly a son. The father didn't know it, but what he wanted was for that trisomic child to earn the role of son. Nature was just a part of the equation. At night, at the bar, he was transfigured by beer and cigarettes, in a Romanesque optimism. He'd memorised the neurological-development sequence, which he began to see as a kind of mathematical formula (the tunnel of the production line), and explained didactically to whoever would listen, how, in no time at all, perhaps in two or three years, his son would be a normal child. He spoke with the same obsessive compulsion with which he sometimes described aspects of the perfection of the game of chess, to which he had been addicted for a short while as a teenager until a defeat had brought on an uncontrollable fit of tears and he had freed himself of it forever. Of course, he explained (wishing there were a blackboard in the noisy bar to make his explanation more efficient), you have to make up for the neurological handicap with over-stimulation. So, while a normal child needs to hear a high-pitched sound just two or three times in order to master its instinctive reaction to it, a trisomic child will need to hear it three hundred times, until nature recovers what it has lost. I've even bought a wooden recorder, he confessed in an almost threatening tone, and I spend the day playing a few notes around Felipe. High-pitched sounds, you see? And he opened another beer. See that guy walking there — see the relationship between the movements of his arms and legs. It looks simple. But in mongoloid children you need to implant this pattern of movements to bring them out of their neurological haze. You have to make up for nature's flaw; fix the manufacturing defect.

Several times a day, in five-minute sessions, the baby was placed on the living-room table, face down: the father on one side; his wife on the other; and, holding his head, the maid, a shy, quiet girl who came every day now. Three serious figures at an operating table. Face down, the baby's head was turned to look at his right hand, which moved forward at the same time as his left leg; left arm and right leg making symmetrical, lizard-like movements, guided by the adults' hands, which were the strings of the marionette, as his head was turned to the other side. There was a cadence in it (one, two, buckle my shoe; three, four, knock at the door), the same as in human footsteps; the tentacular network of the neurological system has to establish cerebral dominance and everything that stems from it, he thought. In the program, it was fundamental to reinforce cerebral dominance

— that is, to establish one side of the brain as dominant. The three of them moved like robots, in those short five-minute sessions almost every hour, when he'd interrupt the book he was writing and head for the production line of his own son. A baby appeared in the book, the baby Jesus, son of a bourgeois vampire, a real-estate shark, who, in 1970, made edifying speeches about kindness, morality, and good manners, while literally sucking blood from the aortas of defenceless young women. His character always took care to put delicate bandaids over the holes made by his canines on the necks of his victims, who fainted. The father closed his eyes: maybe it was the baby who, from his silence, was guiding the rhythmic, almost military gestures of the three adults around him. He remembered a joke about pigeons training humans, and smiled.

In 1975, he was in Germany as an illegal immigrant. He borrowed the money for a train ticket from Coimbra to Frankfurt and disembarked at the *hauptbahnhof* with a few coins in his pocket, an address on a piece of paper, and a sketch of some streets. It was nearby — he could get there on foot. He crossed the beautiful bridge over the Main carrying his backpack, trying to control the panic that was beginning to wash over him. He was having a hard time living out the role he'd given himself of a starry-eyed Marco Polo discovering the world. There he was in the mythical Germany of the books he'd read (Johann Goethe, Thomas Mann, Günter Grass), treading that ground. But fear was omnipresent. If he didn't find work, what would he do? He didn't know a single word in German. He finally reached the immense building of the university hospital (the interminable sequence of letters on the façade suggested it, in bits and pieces) and headed straight underground, as he'd been instructed. He had to see a certain Herr Pinheiro. Herr Pinheiro was a friendly

Algerian who spoke every language in the world. His fear now gave way to a growing euphoria — he'd barely finished enquiring, and he was already being led to a cloakroom, where he was given a white uniform and a locker to stow his things in. He was offered seven marks an hour. He didn't need to say yes — he just smiled. Euphoria. Cerebral dominance, he thought, like a mantra, controlling the rhythm of his son's movements on the table. A slave in ancient Egypt, led, laughing, to row a boat eighteen hours a day in the darkness of the basement (and he chuckled at the image) just for the satisfaction of staying alive, supporting the architecture of his bones, standing, even if it was only for one day more. He was so stupid that he pulled his uniform on over his pants and shirt, and emerged from the cloakroom a ridiculous cabbage, until a smiling woman in the corridor speaking an impossible language explained with brusque but maternal gestures that he had to take off his clothes before putting on the uniform. Finally dressed properly, he entered the giant hospital laundry. Modern times, he remembered, aestheticising life — Chaplin on the production line. Because he felt he was a writer, he was always precariously perched atop his own safe conduct, atop the alibi of his still-imaginary art, a constant observer of himself and others. Someone who saw, not someone who lived.

He scooped up the baby after the series of movements and repeated the silly song he'd made up in an effort to build the image of a father, which he still hadn't found in himself (*He was a teeny-weeny rascally little cutie pie ...*) and put him back on the ground, face down. The idea of time (no, the physical presence of time) is only fully perceived when time itself really starts to devour us. Before that, he would daydream years later, time is nothing more than dates on the calendar; for many years it seems there is stability, a tranquil kind of eternity that slips past in everything we think and do. We defeat time; we run faster than it. If the devil had appeared there, he would have made a pact — and he smiled at the idea. He opened Piaget's book on intelligence in children and tested his son every day — a race against time, yes, but at that point time was still unmoving, which made things easier. If I put this plastic toy on the ground right now the baby will go after it and try to grab it; but if I hide it with my hand or a handkerchief, he'll completely lose interest, as if it has disappeared. He tried it: it was true. It made him happy: a normal child, he fantasised. A little more, and soon the baby would be able to recognise the toy just from its foot sticking out. Maybe tomorrow. Or the next day. There was a reasonable span of time in normality. For now he still couldn't recognise the toy just by its foot — which was normal, he realised from reading the book.

But the training wasn't over. In the corner of the living room, the carpenter had installed the piece they'd ordered: a narrow wooden ramp in the form of a slide for babies, with protection on the sides. A strip of linoleum covered the wooden surface. The surface couldn't be too rough, as it would restrict movement, or too smooth, as it would make the baby slide. Little by little, the living room was becoming a work space; the house, an extension of a clinic. His house, of all places: he who'd spent his life hating doctors, hospitals, treatments, nurses, medicines, illnesses, corridors, death — one thing reminded him of another. He placed the baby at the top of the ramp with his head facing down. Off we go, little guy! The baby's arms naturally stopped him from sliding — but the slightest movement allowed him to move a few centimetres. A concrete situation to help him re-encounter his neurological path had been created; according to his book, the ramp would help speed up the development of crawling with opposing arms and legs, which was the pattern with normal children. It wasn't in the program, but the father placed an intermittent alarm clock at the bottom, at the end of the journey, as added stimulus. The baby couldn't see the alarm clock, but he could hear its shrill sound, which his eyes searched for in vain from the top of his little abyss.

He left him there and went back to his room to write his book. The devil appeared in its pages in the form of an angry advertising executive with a pocket full of credit cards. He made belletrist, virulent speeches against God and the world, and conspired towards the failure of *Essay on Passion*, the theme of the novel. There was a heavy dose of grotesque in the character, an expression of his own ill-resolved cynicism. I must avoid stereotypes, he told himself, thinking out loud and ahead, but he still didn't have a solid-enough alternative mythology; he lived in a world, it seemed, that went to great lengths to encourage mental simplification, which he had to avoid at all costs. Sometimes, he had the distinct feeling that he was being written by what he wrote, as if his words knew more than he did himself. (We don't know everything all at the same time; we move forward burying layers of knowledge behind us, he mused.) He lit another cigarette and returned to the living room — the baby had moved half a metre. He wound up the alarm clock (cheese for the mouse) and raced back to his room: he'd just thought of something he had to get down.

Work in the laundry was mechanical. An enormous iron claw came down with tons of washed laundry and dumped it on a counter, and his job was to separate it quickly — bath towels, hand towels, sheets, pillowcases, each size in a trolley, which, as soon as they were full, were taken to the ironing ladies, who in turn spent their time manually smoothing out the items to feed them into a kind of rotating press that swallowed them and returned everything folded into the hands of someone else, who, with another trolley, vanished through a distant door back into the main building. For the first few days he was fascinated by that assembly-line production and the Babel around him: Yugoslavs, Spaniards, Portuguese, Arabs, Algerians, Turks, Italians. He developed a crush on an Italian girl in the sewing room (the seventh seamstress in the fourth row on the right) and, in their rare, short breaks, tried to approach her, asking for a light for his cigarette. She talked in a lively manner with another Italian, showing her a page in a photo novel, and barely looked at him as she held out her lighter. Her fingers had nicotine stains, like his, and her face wasn't so pretty close up — just her eyes — but he felt happy to see her anyway. He went back to his counter, where another mountain of washed laundry was waiting for him, a little more inspired.

Just five years earlier: it was a recent memory. There was a character who levitated in his book. In his hands, magic realism was corroded by satire and caricature — and, in the end, allegory. Like a Ghandian answer to the stupid violence of the soldiers invading the Isle of Passion in search of communists and pot-smokers, Moisés, thin and pallid as a fakir, rose from the ground and hovered in the air like a hummingbird in a lotus position, until a brutal bludgeoning brought him to the ground, dead, to the relief of the soldiers — *Get that son of a bitch on the ground* was the order they received and fulfilled at the top of their lungs. He stood, euphoric — a fine scene! It wasn't, though — the book he was writing still had no narrative thread. He didn't really know what he was writing, but it didn't matter — he lit another cigarette and gazed at the ceiling. Suddenly he wrote another sentence, his handwriting small on the yellow page. He remembered his son. In the living room, the baby had already made it to the ground and was staring, intrigued, at the clock tick-tocking just a hand's breadth from his unsure eyes. He picked up the little critter affectionately, placed him at the top of the ramp again, and wound up the clock. The struggle to get to the ground began again. The baby's eyes sought the strident alarm going off somewhere in space — he lifted his head and his left arm moved, forcing him to move his right arm, too. He advanced an inch.

His work in the laundry only went until eleven in the morning. From there, he was taken to another sector, cleaning. Wearing a different uniform now, service overalls, he took the elevator with a bucket, mop, and detergents up to the top of the building, and received a brief explanation: clean the floors of the wards and rooms and long corridor. They were paired off and sent to different floors. His companion was a foreigner, whom he imagined to be an Arab or Turk. As soon as they were alone, the man grabbed his arm, pointed at the ground, and said with a hint of threat in the key-word language of immigrants: *'Ich, curridor! Ich, curridor!'* Which meant that from the outset he had the hardest part, going into rooms and cleaning around obstacles. He didn't argue. He walked through the first open door and found a white-haired man with a bunch of tubes coming out of his head. Only his frightened eyes moved, accompanying his movements. His surprise, or fear, seemed to spread across his pale face. There was a set of electronic devices around him, small panels that gave off discreet beeps from time to time — he could hear the old man's heavy breathing. Pull out one of those tubes and he's a dead man, he thought, smiling politely at the motionless figure. The Turk was right: cleaning the corridor was easier. Under one of the machines on wheels, he saw a cockroach scurry towards the bathroom and disappear. Yet the floor was so shiny it was like a mirror. They'll survive the next ice age, he thought, remembering the old saying he'd read somewhere. As he headed for the next room and crossed the corridor, he saw the Turk resting at the end, cigarette lit, his work done. He felt the tension of hostility in his soul: Fucking Turk, he thought, and kept working, walking through each door and finding everything imaginable on the beds: old men and women, sometimes young people, the occasional child, some rooms empty. He couldn't decipher the long words in German, in the corridor, on the wall, on the doors. For a few minutes it occurred to him to study German, an idea he promptly forgot: there was no time. He had to make as much money as he could there. He worked seven days a week, taking on all the extra hours he could.

On a rare Saturday off, wandering around Frankfurt, he walked into a bookshop — thousands, millions of books, all written in German. Going through the aisles, he recognised and took pleasure in a few familiar names: John Steinbeck, Heinrich Böll, Scott Fitzgerald, Sartre, Dickens, Cortázar, Thomas Mann — a chaotic family. Faced with that world he couldn't read, he aestheticised the scene, remembering a phrase by Borges, a tall figure in the shadows, almost an Andy Warhol decal, creator and victim of his own work, his hands in the foreground resting on a cane. 'Supreme irony, God has granted me all the books in the world and darkness.' A statement as elegant and refined as a chess move, amidst tigers in the library, forking paths, and plastic *aleph*s for intellectual consumption. All that was left of God was a literary hypothesis, since all his other meanings were history, he imagined, getting it all wrong — Mohammad was already beginning to loom on the horizon, body and soul. He remembered to look for a Brazilian author and, in his enthusiasm, which then turned into an obsession, he spent hours scrutinising spines and sections — all he found were three titles by Jorge Amado, and nothing else. He was shocked: what had seemed to be a world, that which had somehow shaped his speech and sentences, that which had given him a voice, didn't exist. Step on an airplane, he concluded — and we disappear. We Brazilian writers are small-time sardine thieves, useless Brás Cubas,[†] he almost said out loud, next to the last shelf, while leafing through a beautiful, incomprehensible edition of *Don Quixote*.

The baby made it to the ground once again. This was the most difficult part, and he interrupted his novel to oversee his son in the breathing ritual. He placed the tiny plastic mask over his face, covering just his nose and mouth — a piece of elastic holding it softly to his head. The slightest hand movement would free his breathing — but that in itself was incredibly difficult. The plastic created a vacuum, wrinkling then filling, now fogged with human vapour. It wrinkled again, but more intensely — and once more steamed up with used, hot, spent air. The vacuum was stronger now, a fight for air, the baby's lungs struggling to push beyond their physical limits; and the plastic inflated again, full of a useless, stuffy space that looked like air but was already something other, venomous. The baby's hand groped for the mask to tear it off, a difficult task — there was a chaotic hiatus between the intention and the gesture in itself, which was directionless, while his growing desperation filled and emptied the mask, until he finally managed to free himself of the cumbrance, and his breathing seemed to expand in the happiness of renewed air, the brutal relief, the sudden, violent oxygenation of his brain.

---

† A Portuguese nobleman and explorer, who founded and later became mayor of the village of Santos, one of the first settlements in Brazil.

He could almost see the baby's tiny lungs filling and emptying beyond their limits, now returned to life. Yes, this brutality makes sense, he thought — perhaps (this, he didn't think) the baby really did have to earn the right to be a son. He placed him at the top of the ramp once more and went back to the bedroom, where he shut himself away with the pleasure of his book, lit his cigarette, and (now inverting things) took the never-ending drag that inebriated him, the power of the drug absorbed into every ramification of his soul. He quickly dashed off a few more lines and then looked at the ceiling, sighed, blew out the smoke, and daydreamed.

The following week, another Brazilian, a newcomer, had shown up in the cleaning department — a restless, unpleasant kid. He was tempted to do to the new guy what the Turk had done to him, but he knew he lacked the Nietzschean will for power, at least the more visible kind of power: the hand on the arm, the loud voice, the pointing finger, the puffed-up chest. They divided up the task cordially. In one of the offices, the kid took a table calculator from a doctor's desk and stuffed it in his uniform pocket, saying, 'I'm taking this. No one'll miss it.' In three seconds, he imagined the sequence: the doctor's complaint, the simple checking of the time and floor, the names of the employees responsible and their summary dismissal, perhaps in German, with fingers pointing at the street and a kick in the arse. He grabbed the guy's arm. 'Put that crap back.' The guy dug in his heels, lifting his chin, perhaps less because of the theft and more at the insult of being reprimanded. He insisted, threatening, 'If you don't put it back, I'm going downstairs right now to explain what happened.' The guy smiled. 'It was just a joke, mate! Chill out!' And he let go of his arm: the calculator back in place, a pat on the back, laughter. It was over. No sweat, pal!

He felt nauseated, uncomfortable: would he really have reported him? Pimping on someone was the lowest degree of indignity. The archetypal telltale. Judas. He remembered the tins of sardines and tuna in his pockets, the fear and glancing around, the degrading charade in the dark supermarket aisle, preparing himself for an anonymous pointing finger, cries of stop-thief, the shame, the absolute, irredeemable shame. The problem was that his fellow countryman was an idiot, he thought, justifying himself. Better to work with the Turk — apparently they cut off thieves' hands there, the steel dagger whistling down towards the wrist waiting on a bloodstained trunk, he daydreamed, and finally smiled, writing quickly again in safe, perfectly horizontal lines on the yellow paper — a sign that the text, according to his personal lore, was very good.

Now it was time to take his son into the dark room. At the age of twenty-five his son would still be afraid of the dark (always sleeping with a dim light on) and thunder (he closed every window, louvre, curtain, door, and venetian blind in the house). Maybe, he thought sometimes, years later, it was the fault of these multiple-stimuli sessions. He would never know: time was irredeemable. Nothing that wasn't could have been; make your choice — you've only got one, relax; there's no second chance, there is no other time over this time — he remembered his brother now, as he prepared the slide projector he'd given him precisely for these sessions. He'd photographed shapes (triangles, squares, circles) and objects (nail, chair, book, glasses, orange, tree, teeth, cup), each one with a subtitle in capital letters (*CUP, ORANGE, DAD*). In the dark room, the wall would suddenly light up with an immense close-up of an orange, the text in capital letters, and the father's voice, like that of a drill sergeant, repeating 'orange' (*clack, clack*, another photo), 'tree' (*clack, clack*, another photo), 'key ring' (*clack, clack*, another photo), 'book'. Strapped into a highchair, the baby was distracted by the sudden illuminations, the giant figures on the wall, his father's voice, between one darkness and another. None of it meant anything — just sudden, colourful things shining in front of him — but it had to be repeated several times a day, the random words recited as if in a Dadaist poem.

One day my son will put on those giant glasses and go into the world reading *The Magic Mountain*, dreamed the father, toasting with his drinking buddies. My son will read Ibsen's *An Enemy of the People* (*The strongest man is the man who stands most alone*, he remembered), or maybe he'll be an actor: 'The winter of discontent,' he'd say on stage, thin like his father, dragging Richard III's leg and reciting Shakespeare with the tense discretion of one who really feels what he is saying. Before he'd gone out he'd done Piaget's test — everything seemed fine. *Essay on Passion* was also going well, he thought. Following Hemingway's advice in *A Moveable Feast*, which he'd read in Paris, a wide-eyed provincial visiting all of the special places cited in the book, one by one, and parsimoniously spending the marks he'd earned in Germany (he knew they had to last a while), he always tried to stop the text he was writing at a good place, with the inclination to continue immediately. The rest of the day would be peopled with that desire — and the next day he wouldn't feel the depression of a blank page, a moment of transition, a fleeting block. Never write too much on any given day, he heard himself saying. In fact, write little, respect your readers — if there are any. That was the problem: all the rules in the world and, at the age of twenty-two, he still hadn't written a really good page. Nothing. His time hadn't come yet, he told himself, his mop probing diligently under the beds of the sick, bumping into steel bedpans. His day would come. *All forces were united so the new day would dawn* — he remembered the verse he'd written in his Raskolnikov's attic in Coimbra.

The best part was the night — at around six in the evening he'd head to another underground area of that huge building: the kitchen. The production line was now dishwashing: an immense counter with a conveyor belt — at the end, the altar of the automatic dishwasher. Once again, the Chaplin-like image of modernity was irresistible. Different from now, he thought, his son in mind. There was no irredeemable feeling of suffering or tragedy — life was hard, but full of cheer, and everything was under control, like in Chaplin's gags: at the end, there was applause, not death. A convoy of mini-wagons pulled by an electric car came out of a corridor, manoeuvred skilfully like in a Walt Disney film, and parked in front of the conveyor belt, where employees immediately began taking trays from the wagons and placing them on the moving counter. He'd already done it — the work was similar to that at the laundry counter. He quickly took the trays, placed them on the conveyor belt at the right time, side by side; when one wagon was empty, the car would move forward two metres and there'd be another wagon to empty, and so on. At the conveyor belt was a row of Chaplins, each responsible for something different: cutlery, plates, leftovers and, finally, the tray itself. Down at the end, glasses, plates, and cutlery were placed in the enormous machine, which blew out the hot steam of a tremulous factory — and finally the washed dishes were sent back into the world. The work was non-stop — there was no time to think. But in a rare break, his communist friend whispered, 'The best place to work is on the conveyor belt: have you noticed how Germans throw away food?' It was only then that he noticed: vacuum-sealed portions of salami, untouched pots of butter and jam, toast, bread, everything that came back on the trays was summarily dumped into the rubbish bins. Of course, it was a hospital — and he imagined the bins tossing everything into giant incinerators at another tentacular tip of the building, while the chimneys puffed out black smoke to be lost forever in the skies. But the communists didn't bother with this sanitary zeal. Now working at the counter, he placed a cardboard box at his feet, where he tossed everything worthwhile that rolled past him: salami, butter, bread, toast snacks — dinner was guaranteed. Not least because they'd also received another windfall in this adventure — Herr Pinheiro had granted them, in one of the subterranean ramifications of that labyrinth, a lost room, a kind of deposit, with two beds, a table, and a camp cooker. He and his friend could stay there 'for a while'. Everything was illegal, uncertain, temporary, the week's wages in a discreet envelope, in raw cash, no one signed anything anywhere — but every free day was a fantastic achievement, and the kitchen now provided their meals. They couldn't go out at night because they wouldn't be able to get back in without nametags or documents, but since they only finished work at around ten at night and started again at seven in the morning, all they wanted to do was sleep anyway. He'd never slept so well in his life; work and rest were an endless cycle. They fixed their supper — scrambled eggs with salami, cheese, ham, and butter, all mixed together — and crashed. In the morning there was a row of showers down the hall at their disposal, and in a room with an untranslatable name on the door they found ice in refrigerated drawers. One day we're going to find a severed toe here, they joked, getting ice for their juice, wondering if it was the hospital morgue. Now off to work. We're late.

From the dark bedroom back to the table, for operation

neurological-washing, he joked — not brainwashing, yet. Let's swim, baby: one, two, buckle my shoe; three, four, knock at the door. Five minutes. In the worst-case scenario, he fantasised, his kid would be an athlete. He imagined the next page: Miro, the painter character in *Essay on Passion*, lived at the back of a lost cave on an island — not even he knew what was going on in his head, but what a frightful hurricane swirled there, fuelled by marijuana. All in the name of art: a painting on the wall. The aristocracy of art: true social mobility is this, he thought, his nose discreetly turned up, while his broom swept Germany's floor. Art Liberates: a sticker to put on his forehead. Only then did he realise where the chasm separating him and the aggressive Turk lay; it suddenly dawned on him that he seemed a chosen one in that hospital basement. It began with the kindness of the old Portuguese ladies in the laundry (where it seemed they had worked for generations without leaving the place), bringing him sweet guava paste, wine, bread — the professor from Coimbra, they said, and it was useless explaining to them that he hadn't attended a single class at the university. 'The Carnation Revolution, you know, ma'am.' No, they didn't know anything: they were even forgetting their Portuguese, and they had no way of learning German, but their kindness was the same — middle-aged women straight from the Galician-Portuguese period, shot from the fourteenth to the twentieth century, skilfully moving through the two thousand words of their dialect encapsulated for all time. Then there was the hostility of the legal immigrants, with signed working papers, towards those fucking students who came along with their fair skin and blond hair, as beautiful as Nazi propaganda, and took away their jobs just for the fun of it, bored youths working for next to nothing. They'd leave Frankfurt and go back to their rich kids' lives somewhere in the world:

observe their bearing, their clean hands, their Roman noses up in the air. Even their plans were grandiose: one's an artist and the other one's a doctor, while we (he started to imagine them saying, in the ghetto), we'll be stuck with brooms and scrub brushes until the end of time, because Germans won't stoop to this. Have you ever seen a German here? No, not one, never, they're Alpha Pluses, in another sphere of the brave new world. I'm the most German-looking of all of us here, he realised, looking in the mirror. Maybe that was why, subtly, his work was always the lightest: he was different. Maybe they feel, without knowing why, that I'm going to become a great poet: *All forces are united so the new day will dawn.* Step aside, Turks, he might have said, if he'd managed to narrate his own life; but while he read Nietzsche, it was the Turks who took it seriously. One month later, there was a revolt among the legal immigrants, a Babel-like paralysation of the hospital kitchen. All those incomprehensible voices were shouting around the boss, their fingers pointing at the Brazilians (what was going on?), and he and his communist friend found themselves in the street the next day, not really sure what had happened. 'Inspectors,' Herr Pinheiro explained, shaking his head. They didn't have the necessary documentation. 'Students from other countries can't work there. You understand, don't you?' But he was kind, and gave them a name and address that might come in handy.

From the table, the baby was placed back on his pretend slide, for his slow descent to the ground, which was earned inch by inch, he declaimed under his breath, thinking far. When his wife's maternity leave was up, who would be the third person to participate in the baby's table exercises? 'The parents are not the problem; they are the solution,' they said. He remembered the doctor from the clinic, the last talk — he'd taken a copy of his book of short stories, *The Invented City*, the first he'd published, hidden in an envelope to give her as a present, which he did crushed by shyness, the handwriting of his clumsy dedication crooked. His invincible desire to stake out his territory, to say who he was, to affirm that he wasn't one of the herd, to let her know he knew more than those savages yawning over there — that bunch of dimwits — was accompanied by a vivid feeling of failure, of a book that was bad, unfinished, immature and incomplete: he'd lived so much, but had only written superficial abstractions and imitations, he'd later say of his own stories. And now this son, this silent stone in the middle of the road. There he was, trying to move down the ramp to reach an alarm clock he still couldn't see. But, the day before, for the first time, he'd recognised his toy just by its foot, and wiggled across the floor to pull off the handkerchief covering it. Piaget's triumph! And the father smiled. At the bar, philosophy and laughter, a toast with beer: we are all reiterable! He held out his finger for his son, who had made it to the ground once again, and ran his fingernail softly across the palm of his hand. Soft little fingers immediately clutched his index finger, a tremulous arm poking through the witch's cage looking for safety.

A year later, they moved into a tiny two-storey house in the outskirts of Curitiba. With its area of fifty-four square metres, it was the miniature of a house, which pleased him in some mysterious way. In one of the minuscule second-floor rooms, he made a primitive set of shelves that covered the entire wall and whose boards of Brazilian pine — sanded, painted and repainted, assembled, disassembled, and remade — would follow him for the rest of his life, in perpetual transformation. He liked tinkering with wood. (He sometimes dreamed of a garage space, a work bench, a lathe, a mini–carpentry workshop that he'd never have.) The height and width of the shelves would be the yardstick of how much his standard of living was improving, in subsequent moves, by the amount of wall left over on the sides and above it.

The price of the house was inviting; the repayments were lower than rental prices, and the down payment was a cheque he'd received for a freelance proofing job. Everything seemed easy. They made the down payment on a Saturday afternoon; on the following Tuesday, when they went back to the house, he discovered there was a sawmill nearby and that the noise of the machines, an inextinguishable drone, would accompany every line he wrote. At night, a naked madwoman, blonde as sin, shocking in the moonlight, would sometimes go into the street (a dirt road, lined with vacant lots — they were at the edge of the world), screaming the same unintelligible phrases over and over until someone came to fetch her, bringing a robe to wrap around her, and she'd return in a trance, in her circular madness. He watched it from and within the shadows, mentally transforming the image into a painting by Munch to distance himself — but the hysterical metal of the shrieker's voice hung in the air for hours, resonating. One morning, he discovered that someone had stolen their gas cylinder from the small back patio, cutting the hose that went through the wall into the kitchen. He started buying locks, chains, grating. He had an iron gate put in. In front of the house was a two-by-two-metre plot, which could be a garden. He planted cucumber, sunflowers, parsley, radishes. One afternoon, an elderly lady stopped in front of him and said she admired those who took advantage of the smallest piece of land to produce something. He thanked her — he liked hearing that. He felt (or acted like) like one of William Faulkner's tenacious characters, obeying some ancestral calling that he didn't understand but which he needed to see through by some immemorial force beyond reason. It was a fine literary image, but it wasn't him. He felt on unsure ground; his judgement was still warped by an old umbilical cord attached to his childhood beliefs, the father he'd never had, the Rousseauian dream — get out of this shithole of a city, take refuge outside the system, live in la-la land, establish his own rules, turn his back on History. Not easy — things seemed to be getting out of control.

A troubled phase. His wife had to catch two buses to get to work, which was on the other side of town. Why hadn't he thought about that before? She hadn't wanted to buy the house; he was the one who had insisted, obtuse and smiling. He looked after the house, did some private tutoring, proofed texts and theses. To tell people where he lived, he had to draw them a map, indicating street signs, arrows, names of streets that no one knew. His little street was named after a mediocre poet: Luis Delfino. They didn't have a phone for a good while. Autistic, he immersed himself in the new novel he'd been writing for the last few months, *Ragamuffin*, oblivious to the world, while he tried to publish the previous one. He kept stuffing rejection letters from publishing houses into a drawer, and withstood defeats in literary competitions in silence, but none of it really bothered him. It was as if a part of him was avoiding the unfair confrontation — better to lower his head discreetly and try another corner of the maze. The world was much stronger, more imposing and powerful than he was. The scale of the province had become deeply engrained in his soul. Maybe he should reread Nietzsche, start again, but time had run out. He was beginning to hear the crunch of powerful gears, and a discreet rust was appearing on the things he touched: time was finally beginning to move for him.

And something in his life was starting to be lost. His wife was pregnant again — a high-risk pregnancy, based on her history. A pilgrimage of genetic consultations ensued: if the first case was a simple trisomy, the chances of the syndrome occurring again was statistically remote. But statistics, he knew, were the mere organisation of chaos in a dark room by grumpy employees. An amniocentesis in Campinas removed all doubt: a genetically normal child was on its way. A girl. He had just got the phone call late one afternoon. Through the living-room window, he could see the sawmill across the way, behind the large vacant lot on the other side of the street, which gave the space he lived in a small-town atmosphere. He heard the drone of the machines, which sounded soft to him now, and then the siren to indicate the end of the shift. Six o'clock. The silence that followed was a blessing. He opened a beer, lit a cigarette, and breathed the smoke in deep, his eyes closed, feeling the nicotine flood through his soul: a normal child on the horizon. He was in dire need of a point of reference. I desperately need normality, he told himself, and wondered: where is normality? There was a shortage on the market, and he laughed alone. Not now. With the image of the daughter that he was beginning to absorb, moved, he felt immense happiness.

A joy at such a difficult time. He had never been able to live among others and feel like one of them, and yet it seemed such a simple thing to do. The future was also beginning to weigh in another direction: he knew he was rough, crude, and unfinished, with no resources for survival. How long was his wife going to put up with him? How long was he going to put up with his wife? He'd raised his voice two or three times in his life, always over petty things (he only realised much later); she, never. What was he going to do now that he had finally got his degree? He remembered the old acquaintance who some time earlier had taken him to a shoddy newspaper to try to get a job for his unemployed friend. The newspaper was near the university. He'd climbed the stairs, already peeved to be there, wishing he could just go back to his little house and his book, without speaking to anyone — he felt the seed of depression, which he never really succumbed to. The editor-in-chief was a gruff sort, whose airs were an attempt to disguise his soul hewn from rock. They weren't looking for journalists, but they needed someone to do the paste-up, in that prehistoric year of 1982. No thanks, he said, I don't even know what that is. And he went home. The year before that he'd published *The Lyrical Terrorist*, a novella no one ever ended up hearing about — not even him. Let them wait for the next novel, he thought defensively — all three hundred pages of it.

Essay on Passion was his first self-reckoning, an examination of his own life before his son. It was in the drawer, already accompanied by four or five rejection letters. But he resisted the temptation to play the victim. No one had asked him to write anything. Why don't I think of something else to do? he sometimes asked himself, casting about for a decent occupation.

Literature is the least of my problems, he thought, looking at his son, who, sitting on the floor on a sheet of protective plastic, was trying to eat his own hands — the result was a comic disaster, food everywhere, bean mush on his forehead. But his son would have to do things on his own one day. He'd been submitted to the clinic's treatment to the letter for over a year now: the opposing-arms-and-legs exercise several times a day; the session of words and images; the breathing mask; leaving the baby on the floor as much as possible; all manner of stimuli. But he, the father, was beginning to cave in. It was too much for him. He gave up following Piaget's intelligence-development goals and, from that point on, like lab chimps, who shine in the first few months of life, humiliating human babies of the same age, only to then plateau forever, his son began to fall irremediably behind. He was active, moving all the time (more than was reasonable), but there was something distant about him. He was mysteriously closed off in himself, the insurmountable barrier of a foreign soul that one never got inside. Language was an arduous achievement, terrain in which his son moved forward in unintelligible fits and starts, shards of words and relationships amidst gestures and emotions with no translation. It also took a certain amount of effort to love him, he thought — or didn't think. He, the father, didn't think about anything.

He stationed himself in another sphere for protection, in the tranquil solipsism of his projects. He took photographs of the baby with his Olympus OM-1, his pride and joy. He looked for good angles, those in which his son's face didn't appear to be his own, trisomic, and looked like someone else, normal, like all other children in the world. It was the same for everyone, wasn't it? No one wanted to have their photograph taken with their mouth open, their tongue out (except Einstein, he remembered, and smiled at the irony), their eyes blank, drool on their chin. The eyes. Especially the eyes. Why should it be any different with my kid? He drew his son's face with pencils and fountain pens, seeking a fidelity of lines, and was never happy with the result. He still had a hard time talking about him in public — when anyone asked, he tried to answer quickly, 'Fine,' 'He's great' — and swiftly sniff out a new direction for the conversation. On the rare occasions when he told the truth, always to a stranger, he felt the abyss of mutual discomfort, instantaneous and inescapable. The idea that there were very different people in the world and that they needed less science and more generous comprehension (a way of thinking that now, in the early twenty-first century, seems to be more or less firmly established) was a pipe dream. His son didn't exist, except as an inhabitant of a courtyard of miracles.

Years later, while he was walking down the street with his son, a humbly dressed woman approached him and held out the gift of religion, which he recognised in her tone of voice alone, that plasticky kindness, the innocent smile, false as a gold tooth. 'If you'd like the help of our church, come pay us a visit.' The always-underestimated power of churches, he thought, as he walked away. They'll rule the world again, like mythical comic-book villains. He also thought about how potentially tempting it was for him, the father, to lean on his son, to destroy himself there. To make his son his excuse, an altar of others' pity. Yes, he was a good kid. He had a great future. Shame about the son — it was his undoing. Say no, he told himself intuitively, say no. On another occasion, when his son was still a tiny baby, he had confided his misfortune to a former classmate from university, now running for council as a left-winger, who placed his severe hand, already versed in another kind of theatre, on his shoulder and said, 'The state should do something about cases like yours.' He might have added, 'Vote for me.' Yes, it's true, but I don't like the state, he thought, like a dispossessed peasant or a dispossessing nobleman. The state part I can handle. What I need is a beer, he thought, but he didn't say it.

For many years, even after he had become known as a writer, he was reluctant to talk about his son — it was no longer avoidance, he knew, the adolescent bucking to deny pure, simple reality; it was the brutality of shyness, requiring inexorable explanations unravelling all the way to the depths of a failure. Better to spare others; it was always good to keep one's intimacy intact. The failure is ours, the wingless birds we keep in metaphysical cages, to somehow recognise our own dimension. For a time, he fed on the illusion of normality; he still nurtured this mirage, now as a disguise, that his son didn't stand out in a crowd; he didn't attract attention; he seemed normal. The father needed to shed his fear, however.

Breaking point. The rare moments when life stretches to breaking point, and reaching back is useless because we never get back what's gone. He had his first such moment at the age of five or six: he refused to go fetch three lettuces from the neighbour, disobeying his own dad. 'I'm not going,' he stated clearly, staring him in the eye. And in an even louder voice, testing his own recently discovered strength, he repeated, 'I'm not going.' His dad practically hung him by the collar with one hand and whacked him across the backside four or five times with a piece of plywood that looked like a racket, then let go. 'Aren't you, now?' He bawled his eyes out, perhaps less from the pain and more from the discovery of his own limits. 'I'm going.'

If you want to say no, be prepared to deal with the consequences. He learned the lesson, and spent his life saying no, perhaps to recover from that first failure, and developed survival techniques to save his backside. How hard it was to say no! Another such moment came at the Rio de Janeiro Merchant Navy School, where he went in 1971, following his dream of becoming a Joseph Conrad — to travel the world and write his books, to say no to the university and life in the 'system'. For a few months he experienced the relative stupidity of the school with its tight military regime that didn't let up for one second, from the morning workout to the sentinel shifts at night, with difficult classes practically all day long. He had no regrets; it was a good memory. He made it through the initiation pranks without any major hassles because he was a 'bug' — students from elsewhere were spared somewhat. Brazil was going through the worst part of its military dictatorship, which cast its long shadow across everything. He used his sentinel shifts to read — eclectic in his choices, he remembered reading *One Hundred Years of Solitude* and an essay by Karl Jaspers in intervals between logarithmic tables and his nautical manual. He considered himself an existentialist, without really understanding what that meant. Around him, the morals and logic of Vargas Llosa's *The City and the Dogs* were, in effect, the tragedy of military schools. One of his classmates, nicknamed '2001: A Space Odyssey', jumped out of a second-floor window to escape a prank, and broke his leg. In the inquiry that followed, he didn't turn in the veterans. Another kid, a general's son who grew marijuana somewhere on the school premises, confessed to his classmates that he'd received the answers to the entry exam the day before he sat it. At the same time, he had good friends there: one of them told him what it had been like to participate in a stake-out of the guerrilla Lamarca, in Registro, as a recruit, without understanding a thing. Brazil couldn't be rationalised: it was under your skin and underground.

An apprentice existentialist, he decided the school wasn't his place. He wrote long love letters to a distant girlfriend, and received as many in return, with lipstick kisses to seal in the passion. Playing his family, he asked for money on the one hand while plotting his exit on the other. He discovered he needed his mother's permission to leave — he wasn't old enough to decide for himself. He painstakingly forged her signature on the document (he'd always been good at drawing), and presented it at the counter. With a touch of sadism, the uniformed employee told him he'd relocate him to the army, as he'd have to see out the year in military service. But he presented a document from Curitiba's Training Centre for Reserve Officers (this one real), exempting him from regular military service, to the man's disappointment. The next day, not yet eighteen, he was standing on the busy Avenida Brasil, suitcase in hand, with no idea what he was going to do with his life, except that he was going to be a writer. It wasn't a rational decision, carefully weighed and thought through — it was a kind of growing claustrophobia that burst out of him from time to time to bring about some kind of radical change. There he was now, alone, half of him dreaming, the other half too, and he felt fear surge through his body, arresting his footsteps, as he climbed onto the bus home.

His son started taking his first steps two years and two months after he was born. I was never precocious myself, he thought, smiling, when he saw him walking on his own for the first time, his balance delicate and careful, though firm. His tardiness in learning to walk wasn't a problem; the program actually encouraged this delay so as not to get him on his feet before he was neurologically ready. No walkers, crutches, or external help, considered veritable crimes against the child's development. The longer he spent on the ground, the better. He always remembered an observation he'd heard at the clinic: poor people's children often have much more motor coordination, agility, and neurological maturity than rich people's children. Poor mothers put their babies on the ground and go off to wash the dishes, cook, and work, and their children have to fend for themselves. Rich mothers have generous, perfumed breasts, all kinds of protection against the horror of infection, careful nannies, safety straps, prams, cushioned walkers. The free ground of childhood can be a powerful ally in a baby's neurological development when we aren't afraid of it. *Even if it's not true, it's well told,* he would think twenty years later, when he noticed his son's excellent balance when he walked (he had hardly ever fallen or slipped, always careful and steady in his footsteps) and the quality of his swimming, a thousand times better that that of his father, who was a total klutz and shameful in a swimming pool.

Language, however, was painfully slow. Every day, he rued the uselessness of those words on cardboard, that irrational sequence of random names that he recited aloud on an hourly basis, his son looking on with glassy eyes as his dad showed him the words written in upper-case letters, one by one: refrigerator, daddy, table, chair, pen, whistle. He knew it was useless, but the child's mind had to get something out of the repetition of words — at the very least, some sense of focus. Teaching a child to read when he still couldn't speak? Stupid American pragmatism, he thought, remembering the fragile theoretical apparatus on which the program was based — which, truth be told, was a mechanical technique, blinkered behaviourism, he told himself, as if seeking an alibi for his own tiredness and failure, but what did it matter? It was better than nothing. He didn't even try at least one program — mathematics. In the clinic's magical method, the child was meant to be shown sheets of cardboard with different amounts of red dots on them and the corresponding numbers: 3, 9, 2, 57, 18. By some miracle of mathematical multiplication, the child, without thinking, *would learn* the number of red dots and implant the numbers in his mind, not by rational counting, one by one, but by the volumes, a kind of numerical gestalt. Worse: the program had originally been designed for normal children, he thought. Normal children: that was his nightmare. Why would a normal child need this torture?

It wasn't the program of numbers that he was thinking about now, as his son headed for the door, with slow, but steady steps — he was trying to see if they followed the pattern, the left leg moving in unison with the right hand. They seemed to be, but he wasn't sure because the boy's path was full of obstacles, which he considered carefully as he walked. The father thought about his tiredness and exhaustion, about the end of a line, about his feeling of incompleteness in everything he did, on the threshold of a depression that he refused to accept, looking for a way out. He thought about the lack of a way out, about defeat, precisely now, when he had a beautiful normal daughter, and his son was not intimidated by the world — he arrived boldly at the door, which was locked, raised his hand to the latch and awkwardly tried to open it in a useless, mechanical succession of stubborn blows, still unable to grasp the abstract hypothesis of a key.

Work dulled their wits. After the hospital in Frankfurt, they'd wound up in a small labourers' guesthouse in a satellite town — he could no longer remember the name or how to get there. He remembered a Venezuelan immigrant who, according to legend, had won a fortune in the German lottery and donated everything to the church, carrying on his purifying work of cleaning stairs and corridors with mops, rags, generous detergents, and an interminable, edifying monologue about the advantages of Jesus Christ — a paranoid litany, but with method, and bearable even, if you thought about other things as you worked and also kept a certain physical distance to avoid the habitual soft touch of his hand on your shoulder with each sentence. Because of his good contacts, the man always had an odd job up his sleeve, and in exchange the two Brazilians, the communist and the atheist, exercised religious tolerance to the point of attending a service at his so-called miraculous church. It was better to accept the invitation, they decided, thinking about the comfort of the pension they were in and the jobs coming in practically every day.

He was impressed by the discreet but real wealth in the details of the temple. On a mezzanine at the back, for example, there wasn't an organ or a children's choir, but a glass-enclosed area for mothers with crying babies. Apart from that, it had a Protestant dryness, false Gothic windows, and a smell of fresh paint — and sermons in German with an intonation that reminded him of the priests in Santa Catarina when he was a child. But it really was a German church, from the faces, all Alpha Pluses; they were the only savages there, he thought. This was one of the few moments in his life in which he really beat himself up over the thought that he was selling his soul (how did I get dragged into this shit?) in exchange for work. But he was selling his soul to God, not the Devil; and it was a reasonable price, putting up with the lectures (always somewhat on his guard, his eyes sceptical, eyebrow raised, a resistance that further stimulated the hard work of evangelising the world), and in exchange spending his days doing odd cleaning jobs, paid at the end of the day in nicely counted marks and shiny pfennigs. The comfort of the hospital was gone; now each day was a struggle for them, illegal workers trying to scrape together some money.

On the very first day, they had to be on the pavement outside the pension at 6.30 a.m. — a car would take them to a clinic in another town. When they tried to open the door, they discovered it was locked. They did everything they could to get it open (a glass-and-aluminium door in the kitchen at the back of the building) but it was useless, and the clock was ticking. They wriggled clumsily through the narrow window over the sink, jumped and ran out front, worried about missing their lift. On the pavement, another illegal worker was already waiting. 'How did you get out?' they asked. By opening the door, gesticulated the Arab, stretching his hand out in front of him with a smile: the door opened outwards. The two numbskulls, their wits dulled by labour, had been unable to open an unlocked door out of their sheer inability to come up with an alternative.

He opened the door and his son ventured outside, exploring:

in front of him was the same yellow vee-dub, an object of veneration for the baby. The car door was open and he headed straight for it, ever careful in his footsteps. His father watched him through the window, smoking a cigarette. His feeling of failure came back to him — would his son one day speak, read, write, become civilised? He sensed the brutal reality: as always, he needed to be honest with himself. No, his son would never be a normal child — he wouldn't even come close. He, the father, had had a two-year fever, a temporary delirium of the senses; he had lived under a veil of illusion. The force of theory (not even a theory, but a mechanism of logical connections, in which life was reduced to half-a-dozen stimuli and responses) had supplanted his banal sense of reality. The child didn't seem to respond to his affections; he lived in his own little world — nothing around him really seemed to touch him. Words were brief, broken syllables, more a vocal exercise than the creation of concrete references. But the father still hadn't given up, although his energy wasn't the same anymore — it was his wife who sustained that interminable machine of stimuli, now with a daughter to look after, too. The father, a nomad, ignorant, was already secretly dreaming of a horizon of escape. A rolling stone gathers no moss; he almost recited the stupid cliché out loud when he opened his fourth beer, in the bar, late at night. The first time his daughter looked at him, in the same maternity ward, at the same swinging doors, in the hands of the same unpleasant doctor, at the same hour and with the same dreams in tow, now tattered and scarred, but still dreams, the hard stare of the baby's lively, black eyes pierced those of her anxiety-ridden father — again a cartoon drawing. So you wanted a normal child? Here I am.

The one who needed normality was him, not his children, he would think years later, coldly analysing that game of calculations in which children were cultural and emotional investments, pragmatic projections of his great, genius qualities, under which he remained buried for years. Well, it's easy to be altruistic when your kids help, he counter-argued, for the first time in his life tasting the bile of resentment. But he knew it, he knew what this sour feeling was: it was no longer a desire to cry, to hide, to disappear in the haze of desperation; now it was an unpleasant but active feeling, a desire to stomp on his imaginary enemies, all those bastards who — who what? Who? You're alone, exactly as you had planned, he thought. Even more so now: your childhood guru isn't going to save you or rescue you; his world, that Rousseauian utopia, is in the past, and you don't have anything to replace it with. It's as false as a Disneyland garden. Nature has no soul and, left to our own devices, we'd all be little or big monsters. Nothing is written anywhere. The day that dawns is a phenomenon of astronomy, not metaphysics. You have science, which you've just discovered in nooks and crannies of your Language and Literature course, the delights of linguistics as a portal for looking out on the world, but this has only dismantled your veneration of spring even further — this is the aftermath. You're resentful. You're not a writer yet, but you've always known how to name things. That's your core quality, he thought. The ability to name things. To write is to name things. He couldn't say: to say what things are — because things aren't anything until we say what they are. What thing is my son? Up until now, a mirage, he thought, nicotine in his nerve endings. The smoke he savoured didn't relax him anymore; it was a jab of anxiety and depression that he breathed in, thinking about the power of the chemical, and telling himself that everything is chemistry, we are nothing — which was an excuse, a vulgar alibi.

Yes, we are: there's my son trying to work out the best way

to get up onto the car seat, his hands and feet feeling their way almost on their own, without the help of his head. He thought about stubbornness: his son was stubborn. It came with the syndrome, he knew, the circularity of his gestures and intentions, which he repeated over and over like a record stuck in a groove — but he, the father, was also stubborn, and even more obtuse because he didn't have the excuse of the syndrome. Truth be told, he took refuge in stubbornness; he sometimes pretended he was a tragic character who couldn't avoid doing what he did because his destiny was inexorable, which was an absurd fantasy. He had no faith whatsoever, cosmogony was empty, there was an abyss of time between him and the Greeks — but nevertheless he indulged his tragic delirium: nothing that wasn't could have been. Only the coldness of an outside gaze could give life this dimension. Here, now, he was at the eye of the storm of himself, and life couldn't be made aesthetic; it wasn't, nor could it be, a picture on the wall. Now that is supreme alienation, he thought, reviving a word from the 1960s that had been repeated like a mantra: alienated, alienation. Which, in his diffuse memory, was the opposite of authenticity; authentic man versus alienated man. Ideology was a word people bandied about without really knowing what it meant. The process of concealing reality. How so? The process of concealing *true* reality? Someone would have to explain. Christians and Marxists were in the same metaphysical boat. The true reality was time, the only absolute reference, he mused, feeling his own rust. What was inexorable was transformation: any kind.

Using his arms, his son pulled his body up to the height of the running board of the vee-dub: he's going to make it in, he thought. He remembered one of the photographs he'd taken, of the baby in a blue jumpsuit crawling on the table — beautifully framed, a balance of colours, his face in sharp focus against a soft background. Yes, he looked like a normal child. He, the father, was the one who didn't look normal. He had shown the photo to an acquaintance, at once proud and insecure about his son — he, the father, hoping for the legitimisation of his dream. 'Yes, his eyes really do seem slightly empty,' she had said, as if she wasn't speaking to the father, but to the scientist that he was pretending to be: he would never forget the dry pain in his soul when he heard that stupid but calm observation from someone who also had no intention of going through life believing in or creating illusions. Yes, the eyes. Everything worked poorly in the syndrome. The world he saw was our world. He didn't see the horizon, or the abstract, or the concrete. The world was ten metres in diameter, and time would always be an absolute present, the father would discover ten years later.

I'm also in training, he thought, remembering another publisher's rejection letter. Real life was beginning to yank him violently towards the ground, and he laughed, imagining himself in his son's place, coordinating arms and legs in order to stand in the world a little more steadily. There was a jumbled succession of facts: his trips to Florianópolis for the master's degree he was starting, seeking a future means of survival and way to transform his life, his growing insecurity, his escalating fear of facing a new life, taking a step forward, freeing himself of phantoms. It was a moment of rupture, like others in his life, which always left their mark. The only thing that kept him going was his almost theatrical, bordering-on-ridiculous self-esteem — a primitive, encapsulated vanity that he did a good job of disguising — a crazy certainty about his own destiny, and the very idea (actually, a secret feeling) that there was a destiny. But he had to do something, just in case.

He remembered the first moment in which his dream truly ended. After the dispersal of the actors' community in which he felt paternally protected by his guru, protected enough to exercise his good-humoured, at times uncouth, or even rude anarchy, that of those who feel protected by the idiocy of the group rather than an idea of society — there was a moment of putting into practice the neo-medieval mythology of living on a peasant scale, now on his own. In his case, he was going to be an artisan of mechanisms, a watchmaker. And in a small town, also on a human scale, according to his eternal humanist dream. Hadn't Plato written that the ideal republic would have two thousand inhabitants? 'What was I thinking, in 1976, when I came back from Europe?' he asked himself, unable to understand, years later. Nothing: it had been a dream fuelled by fear. He was, in a way, the same child, bucking to avoid having to face life. Rupture was painting a poetic sign, in homage to García Lorca: *FIVE ON THE DOT* — *Watch and Clock Repairs*.[‡] It was renting a place on the main street, signing a contract, the first in his life. Framing his diploma from the Brazilian Watchmaker's Institute and hanging it in a prominent position on the wall, to the consternation of the other watchmaker in town, who didn't have a diploma but was infinitely better than he was. At the age of twenty-three, having completed high school, a reader of Plato, Hermann Hesse, Carlos Drummond de Andrade, William Faulkner, *O Pasquim*,[§] Aldous Huxley, Fyodor Dostoyevsky, Wilhelm Reich, and Graciliano Ramos, with a book of unpublished stories in a

---

‡ A reference to part 1 of poet Federico García Lorca's 'Lament for the Death of a Bullfighter', in which the line *at five in the afternoon* is repeated over and over.
§ A Brazilian periodical first published in the late 1960s that spoke out against the military dictatorship.

drawer (*The Invented City*), he hung the freshly painted sign over the two-metre nineteenth-century door in downtown Antonina, Paraná, went behind the small counter, arranged his tools, lenses, and clock-winding keys on the table and waited, feeling a cold pang in his stomach at facing the world on his own, hoping that one of the town's three thousand inhabitants would bring him a watch or clock to fix.

His son finally clambered onto the driver's seat, scaling the mountain with the tenacity of a reptile — legs, thighs, arms, and hands clinging to the vinyl as he inched along. The father watched him from a distance: everything was fine, except him, smoking and thinking about the crossroads he was at. He had two whole books in a drawer, and two children, these of flesh and blood; one of them there in front of him, trying to stand up on the seat he'd just climbed. He heard the noise of the sawmill, already part of the backdrop of his life. The turbulence of rites of passage: another moment of rupture. It seemed that now the intervals between them were getting shorter. He was tired, but he still had a lot of energy at the age of thirty — he had to decide what to do with his life, and felt painfully incapable of survival. Money: he needed to make money. He thought about the perspective of becoming a lecturer — he who had never walked into a classroom holding a class list. He was always the one sitting at the back, near the exit. There was a public examination coming up in Florianópolis. If he passed, he'd be one more of the country's millions of public servants. It was for a good cause, he supposed — perhaps a teaching post was the only decent job left in the country, he mused, to boost his own spirits. At the same time, he sensed a life change that he was incapable of verbalising, but he knew what it was: leaving. Not taking any initiative, but allowing the current of life to take him in another direction — to leave his wife, children, home, past; to start over, a new life, once again. Fuck it, he thought, exasperated, feeling claustrophobic, lighting another cigarette and thinking about his beer later that night, while his son, now, was holding firmly on to the back of the car seat, already standing. Money: money had no worth in Brazil; it hadn't for many years. It didn't even have a name any more, that string of zeros, in a silly little Weimar Republic that was lazily governed but had solid, delirious monetary indexation, for those who had any. For those who didn't, like himself, his only option was the bank, where he went to pay an instalment on his house and discovered that, through some economic magic, his instalment had suddenly gone up by almost 200 per cent. There was no longer the slightest relationship between things and what they were worth or cost: it was all thin air. You bought something for one hundred, paid three hundred, and owed nine hundred. What was supposed to have been a housing program for low-income earners was turning into a form of extortion that favoured the upper-middle class, in a scam designed to get the government to subsidise the social abyss; now, in the twenty-first century, everyone had to cough up, he thought years later, trying to understand Brazil's imbroglio.

'This is bullshit. I'm not paying,' he told the bank employee, who zealously overlooked the curse and reminded him of the threat.

'You'll lose your house.'

'So take it.'

Say no, and deal with the consequences. He did the maths with his wife, pencil and paper in hand, hoping for a dignified exit: if it took the bank a year to kick them out, the house would have been a reasonable deal, considering everything they'd invested so far as monthly rent. First he tried to sell it. The best offer was an exchange: a Chevette with lowered suspension, wide tires, aluminium wheels, a Virgin Mary dangling from the rear-vision mirror — everything in exchange for the debt, but he was stupid and thought it too little. Soon, as letters from the bank piled up in the drawer, only busybodies came to see the small disaster advertised in the classifieds. They moved out and lent the empty house to a friend who, with his wife and daughter, sold posters in the street. You can stay until they kick you out; just pay the electricity and water bills. If anyone asks, tell them you don't know where we've gone, they said.

Almost on a new page, now a lecturer in Florianópolis, he got a phone call from his wife: a court employee wanted her, the defendant (after all, the property was in her name, not his, as he had been unemployed at the time) to sign a document. 'But how did he find you? Paulo Maluf is still at large!' he remembered joking.¶ And he went on, 'Pick up Felipe and make him cry a lot! Maybe the guy'll feel sorry for you.' Charles Dickens reread by Groucho Marx.

The bank, of course, impersonal and omnipresent, wanted to bleed them dry, every real or imaginary centavo; the proposed settlement was obscene. People were going to court en masse to fight the extortionate increase (and would win, years later, at the obtuse snail's pace of the Brazilian justice system); but he, the little anarchistic savage, wanting to turn his back on his own ordeal and be done with it, gave up, imagining thirty years in front of him of dealing with papers, lawyers, and every imaginable son-of-a-bitch under the sun whose purpose it was to

¶ A Brazilian politician whose four-decade political career has been plagued with allegations of corruption.

make his life hell, with debts piled up that might even come back against him sometime in the future, all for a shitty little house that was completely worthless. He discovered that all he had to do was hand over the property — a sort of 'payment in kind' was the magical legal requirement for what had been obvious ever since the Code of Hammurabi: if I cannot pay, I will return it as I received it. Maybe in the past they cut off debtors' arms so they'd learn their lesson, but now all one had to do was remain poor. He typed up the proposal himself, with writerly touches, transcribing the law to a T. He almost signed off with: 'And go fuck yourselves.' The problem he had idiotically created all by himself three years earlier, one Saturday afternoon, faced with the real-estate agency's irresistible offer, was finally resolved for good. The house, now in the hands of the bank, would finally return to its real market value, outside of the country's monetary insanity — if the bank wanted to sell it.

His son finally reached the steering wheel of the car and twisted it, first to one side and then the other, imitating his father, until he discovered the horn. He started honking. Pleased with his discovery, he honked non-stop. His father went over to him. 'Felipe, stop it.' He didn't listen — just honked and hollered, his left hand steady on the steering wheel. His father tried to get him out, delicately at first. 'Felipe, look at me.' His son was strong — the early stimulation had worked. His hand was firmly clutching the steering wheel. He stopped honking, and now held on with both hands. He didn't want to get out. Slightly empty eyes, the father remembered, and felt irritated. The cumulative dimension of failure, he might have thought if he'd been able to, but he was on the other side of the same wheel they were clutching. Stubbornness: he couldn't get out of his own world, which at times spiralled into a circular compulsion, like now. It took strength to get him out of there. Father and son were alike, mirroring one another in that brutal, absurd instant. His son started honking again, looking straight ahead, a pretend driver in a mental race in which perhaps he saw himself as an adult; and the adult, a child, didn't see himself, as he tried to get his son out, a little more violently now. He pulled him by the waist, but he held on to the steering wheel and kept honking, banging on the horn to place his hand back on the wheel, making engine noises with his mouth. He sank his foot between the seats to steady himself better, and went back to honking. The father tugged at him roughly, but the boy didn't let go of the steering wheel, his fingers like claws. First, he looked at his father as if he were seeing him for the first time in his life. He looked surprised by an incomprehensible world, a meaningless but tense face in front of him, a surge of electricity that certainly reached his cloudy soul, but he didn't let go; he hung on to the steering wheel in absolute desperation. There was no longer any reason to get him out (chance was, he wouldn't honk again), but his father had now entered the circularity of his own desperation. Getting his son out of the car was a question ... of what? There was no logic to any of it. 'Get out of there!' His harsh voice was a last barrier before the gesture to come, against he who stared at him without recognising him, who was incapable of verbalising anything; he was incapable. But he hung on to the steering wheel, his empty eyes staring into the full eyes of his father, who finally exploded — as if his own father's hand were there again, resuming the cycle of violence that had to be fulfilled by some divine order, the father's order. He smacked his son — one, two, three, four times — until he finally let go of the steering wheel.

Indocile in the arms of his father, who hightailed it out of there as if fleeing the scene of a crime, the boy stared at his father's face, which remained meaningless. He didn't cry. After he was out of nappies, his father never saw him cry again. At the most, his face showed irritated surprise at something incomprehensible, a diffuse reaction that quickly faded and was replaced by something else of immediate interest in front of him, as if each instant in life suppressed the previous one.

Back in Coimbra, he held the plump envelope up to the light, trying to decipher its secret. He patted it before opening it, as there appeared to be something different inside. Money: it was a 100-dollar bill, protected by two sheets of folded paper, together with a letter from the brother-in-law who had financed his trip to Portugal and would finance his return to Brazil, fourteen months later, with a Varig ticket paid for in twelve instalments. The world was so serene then that you could step off a plane in Europe with just a one-way ticket and a few dollars in your pocket. Or with nothing even. A few years later, he would learn that the marvellous 100-dollar bill, and the others that came on a monthly basis to cover his rent at the pension on Rua Afonso Henriques (which he, a good Samaritan, faithful to his mission of Franciscan poverty, would exchange for escudos at the bank rather than at an exchange bureau, to help with Portugal's reconstruction after the Carnation Revolution, in response to a request by one of the interim governments of 1975) had come directly from the private stash of a São Paulo politician, an old-school kleptocrat with a secret safe at his mistress's flat. The mistress had inadvertently revealed the location of the treasure to someone with a keen ear, like in a good spy movie. The revolutionary operation set up to 'recover the people's money' included members of practically every clandestine organisation in the country, among which was the group MR8, opposed to the dictatorship, in which his brother-in-law was active — contraband weapons were stockpiled in the roof of his dental surgery in the west of Paraná State to be used in the event of a fresh outbreak of guerrilla fighting that would bring down the guerrillas of the right and instate the long-awaited Brazilian socialist nation. Along its convoluted path, as it was subsequently carved and divvied up, a small amount of the money had gone to that smaller cause, and a few stray notes, unaccounted for at the time, had ended up in the hands of the lumpen writer of Coimbra who, ironically (or out of fidelity to his alternative neo-hippie mission), didn't believe in any kind of armed solution for anything in life.

In the bookshops of Coimbra, without censorship and freed of an almost millennial dictatorship after a white revolution in Portugal, but with thousands dead in its African backyard, he leafed in disbelief through the *Minimanual of the Urban Guerrilla*, by Marighella (who, thirty years later, by fluke and twists of fate, would inspire commandos of semi-literate drug-dealers in Brazil's big cities). At the cinema, he watched films such as *The Decameron*, by Pasolini, and *State of Siege*, by Costa-Gavras, which were banned in Brazil. One scene in *State of Siege* showed a lesson in torture with the Brazilian flag in the background; one of the cadets being taught couldn't bear what he was seeing, and left to go and throw up. There appeared to be a general dumbing-down, in which governments acted as irrationally as people, and people acted with the rationality of governments. Nobody was outside of this mesh, but everyone was exasperatingly limited in their understanding of all the variables of the present.

One of the distant extremities of the infernal machine now shone in his hand, in October 1975; a 100-dollar bill that had gone from the hands of some contractor to the pocket of a governor, who put it in his safe, and from there, according to the operational logistics of the liberating raid, involving someone who would become minister of state thirty years later, passed into the hands of organisations in Chile, piling up with other 100-dollar bills under the control of other revolutionaries. Part of this war booty was shipped out in green bags to Algeria, while another part went to Argentina, from where, hidden in the militant soles of a Brazilian general's exiled son, it trudged in instalments to the town of Medianeira, where an anonymous dentist would have the revolutionary task of exchanging them safely for Brazilian money and forwarding them to São Paulo and Rio. Five or six of these notes strayed to Coimbra. Happy, with the impossible innocence of one of Sartre's characters, the future writer examined them against the light when they arrived every month (someone had told him that if they weren't false, a translucent image should appear, which he never saw), until his return.

Which didn't take long. When the University of Coimbra finally reopened its doors to new pupils after the 'reckoning'** that followed the Carnation Revolution, in January 1976 he attended a few chaotic classes with two hundred students in enormous amphitheatres — and once again had the claustrophobic feeling that he needed to breathe elsewhere. He suddenly hated Coimbra. Out of the blue, everything there seemed bad for him — especially his brutal loneliness. He was tired of foreigners. Even the Portuguese accent got on his nerves, as did the heavy conservatism, the women dressed in black, the slime of the

---

** The Portuguese term *saneamento*, or 'cleansing', refers to a period of public outcry and reckoning with officials and supporters of the old regime.

Middle Ages, the clichés of the left. The clichés of the right. There he was, alone again, standing metaphorically with his suitcase on Avenida Brasil, taking the bus back.

Years later, again uncentred, free of the house debacle and living a new, solitary life in another city, he was separated from his son for two years, the divided family getting together only on weekends. Nothing was verbalised, but he felt that his still-stable life was hanging by a thread. Perhaps he was the one who needed treatment, not his son, he mused again. For the first time, at the age of thirty-four, he had signed working papers and received the same amount of money at the end of each month. He was a public servant — the secret dream of nine out of ten Brazilians. He experienced the brief euphoria of one who had finally surrendered to the system, tasting a little stability and respectability as he stood in front of the blackboard. He believed he had a few things to say — not about the world, but about the forms of language. Not for long, however. He'd barely begun to teach when what felt like an interminable strike dragged on for one hundred days in the last military government, which he used to write *Tentative Adventures*, his third unpublished novel, which went onto the pile in the drawer. He finished in four months — the quickest book of his life. The publishers' rejection letters were also quick — and also piled up in the drawer. At night he drank beer, laughed a lot, as always, and called editors sons-of-bitches, the lot of them. On weekends he visited his family. In Curitiba, his son was going to crèche with his daughter, and the social contact was doing him good. The gruelling training of his son's early years had been left behind, but it had done some good: the boy was in good health, his footsteps were steady, his posture was reasonably good, his social interaction was great, and his good humour, endless. The problem was that he couldn't sit still.

But one had to get to know him, feel him. Whenever he could, in the little time they spent together in those two years, he talked tirelessly to his son, verbalising everything he was doing at any given moment. Perhaps, he hoped, by the magic of the sound of the words he heard, the child would absorb some seed of language that nature still hadn't given him, like Monteiro Lobato's doll character Emília, he remembered (and retold the story), who was given a talking pill and never stopped talking ever again. He observed his son and tried to understand that other solitary voyage before his eyes. Those subtle, mysterious ties with the world around him: that was what was missing. A perception of others, a sense that there were other living beings around him, the intonations of the world, our silent analysis of figures moving on life's stage in order to find our own place as actors — there was something exasperating missing in his incomplete son, who was like a machine that never stopped moving, at once obtuse and gracious in his contact with the world. Not to mention tireless — he'd knocked over the TV twice, luckily without breaking the tube.

Someone told the father to consult a speech therapist. He didn't put much faith in them — charlatans who invented theories to justify themselves. In his usual self-sufficient stubbornness, he thought it was useless skipping stages if the child still didn't have the neurological maturity for speech; voice training had to be a conscious activity, rather than mechanical; he was even resistant to the idea that speech therapy was a science — most likely it was the mere application of a technique, which in his son's case was useless. The father was irritated, which was becoming more and more common in this phase of life. Late in the day, he and his wife took the boy to the speech therapist and watched a session, which was practically torture: the boy refused to obey, didn't concentrate, didn't listen, and always had something unexpected up his sleeve to change the direction of whatever he should have been doing. The father was irritated because he no longer had the patience for all that bother, which he thought devoid of meaning. The things they say we have to do, and then we go and do. His old feeling of shame, which he thought he was over, came rushing back — all it took was being with his son in the presence of a stranger. That's how the mechanism of isolation begins, he thought. From Monday to Friday, in Florianópolis, he practically forgot he had a son — it felt good, although he didn't think about it. It was as if he was happiest on his own; but, truth be told, he felt as if he were in a strange limbo, living nowhere at all: none of his projects had resulted in anything, book after book; even his idea of building an alternative house on a property he'd bought for peanuts in a community overlooking a beautiful lagoon in Florianópolis started to crumble due to a series of small incompetences (actually, he didn't know it yet, although his soul did, but that wasn't what he wanted). He carried on with the vague idea of a ghost of himself, nurturing his Rousseauian dream again, but with the small advantages of an anxious middle class that simulated contact with nature (he imagined his son happily growing up on a green Walt Disney lawn, a tricycle in the garage, his little friends friendly and understanding — rather than little monsters in the rough, as he would discover a few years later when a street kid collecting rubbish ran away in fear at the sight of the strange, smiling boy who left his parents and walked over to him with his hand out in greeting), a more primitive life, a more communitarian ideal. He repeated the ready-made clichés, delving into the cinema of the 1980s, when the fringe artists of ten years earlier had started making money and, like God creating the world after an eternity of silence, finally thought it all very good. Everything was false, but he still didn't know it, drifting along as he always had; the only real focus in his life was writing, now a form of escapism, a desperate gesture so he wouldn't have to live. He slowly began to be corroded by books, which tried to give him what he couldn't obtain by other means, which was a place in the world; every book was an alibi, a certificate of substitution — the only solid thing he had left was an academic career that he was starting to find petty, small, irrelevant, a dead-end. It was a giant state-run apparatus of knowledge, ironically consolidated by the dictatorship (which everyone would soon miss because they didn't know what to do in a free world), educating people to obey unions and sinking, year after year, into an unbelievable lack of imagination. But he knew, in his obsession with the truth, that the problem was his, the lack of concentration was his, and the failure was his, and his alone.

There he was with his idiot son, staring at the speech therapist. He almost forgot he had a normal daughter who also needed him, perhaps much more than his son did — but all that normal children needed was water, and they grew like weeds, he imagined. It was as if he first needed to find himself again (his old alibi) before he could take care of others. The problem was that he didn't have time for anything or, to put it another way, the only thing that happened was time, nothing else — the feeling was overwhelming. 'He doesn't concentrate much,' said the speech therapist, and the father almost dragged his son out of there. In the corridor, he thought he could feel other people's piercing looks as he yanked along a shameful little creature, incapable of repeating two or three words in a simple sentence. (Nevertheless the boy hugged him with almost complete abandon, as if giving himself up to nature with his eyes closed.)

It was growing dark: a cold, busy Friday. He felt like a cartoon character again, but humourless now. His old car, that yellow pile of shit, took ages to start. His wife said something that he — obtuse — ignored. He felt a poorly digested rancour in his soul, a discomfort under his skin, a mortal desire to run away. In the back seat, his son was finally quiet. He remembered (and the mere memory made him feel even more fraught) the night he had almost died under the wheels of his own car, as if conspiring against himself. Arriving home drunk, he'd gotten out of the car to open the gate. The hand brake hadn't been properly engaged, and the car had started rolling backwards. He'd run back, opened the door, and stuck his foot in to step on the brake, but he'd tripped and fallen. With one leg inside the car, the other out, he'd been dragged on his back across the asphalt, without the strength to free himself from his own trap. His wife (who didn't drive) had jumped from the back seat (where their baby daughter was) and managed to hit the brake with her foot. His back was already bleeding, his shirt torn on the asphalt. There was no one in the street who could have helped him stop the car, which gained speed as it rolled backwards — he felt a chill in his stomach, imagining himself killed by the runaway car. It's that easy, he thought, irritated, as if he'd lost a battle, feeling the profound discomfort of one who couldn't bear the simple idea of a single scratch on his image. The scratch was now in his flesh itself, abrasions, blood, pain — nothing too bad, but he was too delicate. That hurt. He remembered walking into the house and shouting a rosary of curses against everything, especially the ones he'd learned in Germany from the filthiest-mouthed Spaniard he'd ever met in his life: *Me cago en Diós, en la Santíssima Trindade, me cago en la hóstia …*[††]

[††] Spanish for 'I shit on God, on the Holy Trinity, I shit on the communion wafer.'

He didn't know it yet, but now, manoeuvring to get out of that dark parking lot, in the heavy silence that he himself had brought on, he was nearing another landmark moment, of the unforgettable kind that — because there is absolutely no reason for them — act as milestones in life and give it some kind of reference. On the drive back, as he waited to turn onto another road, he allowed the cars with right of way to pass before pulling out. Someone behind him honked, for slightly longer than was reasonable, and he closed his eyes and leaned over the steering wheel. *I'm going to kill that piece of shit.* He heard the horn again, now ostensibly aggressive. He took a deep breath — cars with right of way kept passing; there was no way he could move forward. A gap appeared, but it wasn't enough; his vee-dub didn't have enough torque, and he always allowed a big space so he could pull out safely in situations like this. Now the honking was frenetic. He opened the door (his wife said something, no doubt sensible, that he didn't hear) and went over to the honking car. He discovered that the driver was an elderly man in a suit and tie, now visibly shaken at the sight of the young thug who'd appeared on the offensive in front of him. He didn't see it, but his son had his face pressed to the back window, watching his father's every move with profound attention. This was something that the boy absorbed through his pores, unlike the speech therapy: he took in every gesture, drank in his father's intention, assimilated his aura, eyes wide open in unconditional admiration.

The father, nearing boiling point, leaned towards the window as the man recoiled in fear, clutching the steering wheel, and panted, 'Why don't you take your horn and shove it …' and he let fly with a string of unbelievable expletives in a very loud voice so the son-of-a-bitch would get out of his car. 'Come here, you dickhead!' He wanted to kill him. He thought about grabbing the old guy by his collar and hauling him out the window like in a cartoon, so he could kill him. 'You're very rude!' the man stuttered — an absurd, ridiculous thing to say, his voice cracking, almost infantilised, which was disarming; the father felt as if he'd suddenly returned to the arena of civilisation, in which people exchanged arguments, deliberations, thoughts, and abstract equations rather than punches. 'You're the rude one, you ...' he said, and the swear words came back to get his blood boiling again, while the man finally took his hands off the steering wheel, taking advantage of a second in which the father pulled his head back, and quickly rolled the window up to isolate himself from the monster who wouldn't stop threatening him. Other cars were honking now, piling up behind them; some pulled out of the queue and overtook them, yelling. There was a kind of gorilla frenzy at dusk, all beating their chests and roaring, each with a car in his hands. His head started to cool, and the writer went back to his vee-dub defeated by the ridiculousness of his own actions, his soul plummeting to zero while he tried to cling to a few shreds of argument to justify not what he'd done, but his fucked-up life, with its crooked mechanism of absurdities. He didn't have time to think — he suddenly realised that his son had started shouting 'shit' (with an articulatory efficiency that the speech therapist had been unable to drag out of him) to whomever was closest to his window — driver or passenger — in the succession of traffic jams along the avenue. He pulled the car over into the first empty space, took a deep breath, turned to the back seat, and tried to explain that he shouldn't do that, but the boy was too worked up to listen. He had to wait a little, look him right in the eyes, and hold his face with both hands. 'Look at me, Felipe,' he said, then repeated that he shouldn't do that. 'Daddy was wrong, son,' he confessed, in a small voice. He told him several times that he shouldn't do that. His son finally calmed down. There was a plastic car on the seat; the boy turned away from his father, picked up the toy, and gave it his fullest attention, babbling dialogues that were incomprehensible but calm, while he drove the car slowly up and down his leg.

His son and daughter went to the same crèche, which was great. They came and went together. Life seemed to have found another point of stability, now that the father was back in Curitiba. Six years after it had been written, *Ragamuffin* was finally published in São Paulo by a big publishing house, and was well received by the critics — and the turbulent conditions in which it had been written no longer existed. Although he wouldn't have admitted it if someone had asked him, he was now perfectly integrated into the system, at least into the knowledge-production system that the university represented. As if life really was imitating art, he was becoming the university lecturer Manuel in his own book, cultivating a belly, discovering the pleasures of socio-linguistics and the flavour of routine. Routine was an extraordinary mechanism for generating stability, and a basic condition for emotional and social maturity, he would say, years later, thinking not about himself but about his son. The boy's daily routine provided him with a tranquillising axis. He still hadn't acquired the difficult notion of 'yesterday', 'today', or 'tomorrow' — life was an unredeemable perpetual present, like in a T. S. Eliot poem, but without its charm; time was an anxiety-free 'thing in itself', the immediate space in which he moved, and nothing else. Like with building blocks, in the sequence of facts, events, and things

147

to do that began again every day due to his mother's spirit of organisation (not his father's), Felipe was beginning to learn and discover, more and more clearly, his limits.

An illusion of normality installed itself, which stopped him from thinking about his son in more depth. The crèche he attended was for normal children, the sons and daughters of a certain more-or-less evolved urban middle-class who could afford it and who had a list of humanist good intentions in their pockets. From the ages of four to six, Felipe interacted with other children of the same age, with no major traumas. By now, of course, a well-articulated discourse about understanding differences had begun to make its presence felt — fostering, year after year, changes in the way society perceived those who were different or marginalised. The phenomenon grew consistently throughout the last twenty years of the twentieth century, at least in bigger cities and middle-class environments. At any rate, the civilising agents were always schools, even for the wealthy, who, in Brazil, seemed to correspond perfectly to the image they had acquired over five centuries: the country's elite was visibly unrefined, often grotesque, frighteningly ignorant, incorrigibly corrupt and corrupting, and intrinsically installed in all of the country's mechanisms of power, which in turn were enmeshed at the other extreme with criminality in its pure state, he declaimed to himself, while worrying vaguely about the destiny of Brazil's public universities at union meetings that were almost always stirred up by inept banners, made professional by belligerent unions and incompetent teaching staff.

He examined his payslip at the end of the month in which he went on strike, and followed, with some enthusiasm, the achievements of the 1988 Constitution, trying not to think too much either about those who fluttered around the pulpit of the evening news, all familiar old faces from the era of the dictatorship, or the ridiculous pomposity of their speeches — all of them left or right (terms that hadn't meant a thing for decades, which was actually good, he had to admit), which didn't seem to be about anything. Not exactly: although everything had gone wrong for the country, everyone had a clear idea of what they wanted, and he was surprised to see that they actually got it years later. The only idiot there was him, it seemed — more than his son, who, after all, didn't have the gift of comprehension. The 'national political pacts' made every six months, in which everyone agreed, were always to defend the state and its apparatuses, and the country dug its heels in decade after decade and stayed put — and when it did move, it was backwards. There were medieval crusades for agrarian reform, a revolt of the cocaine-dealers to the rich, Brazil's legal system and police eternally taking inspiration from the Canudos massacre,[‡‡] 'alms-coupons' spearheading the country's social policy — but none of this was visible yet in the late 1980s. As a lecturer at a federal university, he was entitled to monthly transport assistance in addition to his salary (in the form of metal bus-tokens in a plastic bag, which he observed, intrigued, but refused to accept, poor but proud, because he lived nearby and came and went on foot, as if it were a personal problem between him and the government) and food coupons, and thought it good and normal. A beggar's spirit embraced the country — everyone, rich and poor, held out a hand; some wagged their tails. Lecturers retired under the age of fifty with full salaries and perks, and immediately went to work in private institutions in order to double their earnings, when they didn't

---

[‡‡] The War of Canudos (1893–1897), in Brazil's north-east, came to an end when a large Brazilian army force overran the village of Canudos and killed most of its inhabitants.

apply for new jobs in the same university from which they'd just retired — and he finally began to think that it wasn't fair or good. But everyone felt the optimism in the air. The endless power of lies was sustained by an invincible willingness to accept them as the truth.

It was what happened to him too when he thought about his invisible son. The normality of the crèche reassured him. He was still unable to talk about the boy with others; in the obscurity of Curitiba's comfortable solitude, good new friends with whom he interacted or corresponded regularly went for years without knowing he had a son with Down syndrome — the term that, finally, in a sign of the politically correct times, had supplanted the infamous 'mongolism' for good. Two forces seemed to be at play in his silent suppression of the truth. One of them was good, old-fashioned shame — children would always be the measure of their parents' competence, the implacable yardstick of their quality. Yes, of course, in his case there was the genetic alibi (poor thing, it wasn't his fault), but it didn't seem a good-enough excuse; his son diminished him; he was mortally proud of his own qualities, taking strength from them, seeking refuge in them, although in silence. What good was knowing that 'it wasn't his fault'? The fact that he was a man of letters, evolved, filled with humanism and civilisation, didn't make any difference — writer that he was, he was emotionally more insecure than his son, who was actually growing up under good tutelage.

As with everything in life, the father would have said, if he'd thought about it (which, being autistic, he didn't), it is not motivations that are judged, but results. There was a giant, interminable horse race under way. You're a part of it, galloping, he told himself. From morning to night, every day, you gallop. Yes, of course — people understand. People are all decent and will understand. The second fear that silenced him was precisely that: pity, which fuelled corniness, a sticky, caramelised kind of lie. A metaphor — not to say what couldn't be said any other way, but to hide what could be said matter-of-factly, the thing-in-itself. A thing-in-itself: sometimes he thought about it: what on earth am I? And what about Felipe? Who is he and how can I get to him?

The stubbornness of the syndrome was beginning to ease. Slowly, the weight of civilisation, a mysterious set of invisible rules constantly reminding us of the whole dimension of the presence of others that must be respected, even if we don't know why, or against our will, was beginning to influence his son's actions, as he began to weigh (in some dark corner of his mind) choices between options. It struck him that his son no longer did things because he couldn't have done them otherwise, but because he chose to do them; he was capable of choosing them. And, he sighed with relief, his son's choices seemed better and better. His repertoire was still small, his options few, but he was clearly aware of an authority that he had to carefully consider before acting — a yardstick for measuring his own footsteps, which were, as it were, increasingly steady.

His son had been taking swimming lessons since he was practically a baby, and he was good at it. Of course, in real life, everything became a competition. At swimming events, meets, and competitions for people with special needs (almost always disorganised, always hours behind schedule, making the party — which had the magical power of lifting the children's self-esteem — into a little living hell of relatives desperate to disguise the malaise of that patio of miracles, where everyone smiled cheerlessly, milled around chaotically, praised one another tensely, and cheered insanely at the top of their lungs for their exceptional children in the name of the Final Victory, the Big Triumph), there were their children learning the rules of the perpetual horse race, which they had a hard time understanding, but whose nature they immediately assimilated: you had to win.

Maybe it was just him, the father, who was irritated by that inside-out spectacle. Maybe everyone was really happy about the meets; or, more likely, they were all reasonably OK about it when they were alone and really did want the social communion that the competitions represented. But when they found themselves all together in the stupid echo of the gymnasiums, something was lost: the imaginary thread that connected them faded, and their laughter lost its reference and meaning, and became dislocated grimaces on their own faces. There was his son, swimming in the second lane, slow and systematic; maybe he, the father, was the only one in a bad mood, seeing things that weren't there, and it was just a gathering of families with problem children that well-meaning teachers had organised for the benefit of everyone. There was his son, swimming, calmly following the rules. He was incapable of truly understanding the abstraction of the competition, its implicit idea — here, the father was beginning to discover the power of theatrics in the civilising gloss. Long, long before the idea came the gesture — just as tone of voice reaches the ears (and soul) long before a word's meaning and reference. In this pantomime, his son was an actor without a director, but one who respected the rules.

When the race was over, Felipe celebrated like a winner — even when he came in last, arms in the air, as happy as Larry: he was the Champ. The first few times his father patiently tried to explain to him, 'Son, you took fourth place; there are six lanes, you see; only the first one in is the champion.' But halfway through the explanation, the ludicrousness of it all started to contaminate his voice. If his son couldn't count to ten (strictly speaking, he couldn't consciously count over five — he only repeated memorised names, sometimes getting the sequence right), what could 'fourth place' mean to him? It was just a game or, better still, it was the re-enactment of a game, in which, if the boy reproduced what was expected of him (swimming from here to there), he'd be given the champion's cup. Wasn't that how it worked? If he'd swum the distance, 'Why not?' his son would have asked — if any of this absurd, delirious logic actually made it into his head, in pure osmosis with the present moment. He took a good look at his son, both of them impregnated with the phantasmagoric agitation of the gymnasium, where everyone seemed to have something to do at every instant, in a series of races whose participants' names were repeated over loudspeakers that at times were deafening, reverberating. 'Did you enjoy the race, Felipe?' The boy smiled. 'Look! Look! I'm the Champ!' And he displayed his arms and biceps still dripping with pool water, as if it were a wrestling match. 'I'm strong!' he added happily. The next day, unless he was reminded, he wouldn't remember a thing, his eyes glued to a cartoon or his hands busy with building blocks, babbling some narrative around his impregnable silence.

Happiness. The father had always been afraid of this word. When taken seriously, it sounded arrogant; when used casually, it was worn out from overuse, and no longer corresponded to anything except a TV ad or a calendar picture. He was fuelled by good cheer, a sentiment that came easily to him — such that at times he wondered if the idiot wasn't him, rather than his son, for using his abilities and competence so poorly, for petty things. To maintain his cheer, however, reality-avoidance techniques were necessary, or everyone would pay. The illusion of normality that the crèche afforded him lasted a few years. If he didn't think too deeply about it, the boy seemed to correspond perfectly to what was expected of him — in contact with other children of his own age who, no doubt, understood him, or at least assigned him to the world of normal things we deal with on a day-to-day basis, with no major hassles. He was able to switch off from his son, he thought. When the boy was about to turn eight, however, the crèche started sending subtle smoke-signals — a meeting with the parents, veiled hints, supposedly optimistic insinuations, all of which he did his best to ignore while his wife researched other possibilities, which he refused to think about.

The territory of imaginary normality had come to an end — his holidays were over, but he didn't know it yet. Conveniently autistic, the father didn't grasp what was going on when the headmistress said she wanted to talk to him face-to-face, her voice serious. She had already dropped several hints, but he didn't seem to understand what she was trying to say — and she didn't want to come out and say the thing in itself, because perhaps it wasn't politically correct. (Maybe she was afraid of a lawsuit, it occurred to him, years later, a phantom penny dropping.) It would have been better for her if he'd understood and, with deference and thanks, willingly taken the child somewhere far away; but since he didn't understand, she'd have to come out and say it.

First, the subterfuge: 'No, he's not adapting ... Yes, they're starting a new phase, learning to read and write ... Yes, of course, he's great, but you see, the other children ... Well, his inability to sit still, you know? ... Of course, of course, all these years, things were going OK, but it's a job for a specialist. We don't have the structure. He ...' and the headmistress had a certain difficulty looking the father in the eye. Maybe she was at exactly the same crossroads herself. Maybe she thought: *We need a better world, but I can only come this far. Unfortunately. I'd really like to be able to take a leap forward and create a space in the school in which everyone is equal, but I have to respect so many limits, or I'll go crazy. It's something for the private sector.* Perhaps she had on the tip of her tongue the sentence that would finally destroy the delicacy of their civility and bring things to the ground they'd always been on: *We've already done a lot to look after him thus far. Don't be ungrateful.* But instead she smiled and said, 'I've already spoken with your wife. There are great special schools.' He wasn't ungrateful — just a little gruff. He refused to thank her. And now he was having a hard time looking her in the eye. He had to go to the other side of the barbed-wire fence, taking his son by the hand — that territory in which the boy had spent four, five, six, seven years wasn't his. Leave. Intruder. Human community has very clear limits, he thought, exaggerating the bad feeling — a good tactic. Attack, even if only mentally. Play the victim. You wish you'd called her a bitch, but you didn't. Look: you aren't the victim. You've had every opportunity to think about this, and you kept putting it off until the last minute, when you finally heard what you didn't want to hear. It was the way she did it; what got me was the way she did it.

He was still squirming, grasping at straws; there was always the hope of communion — a medieval miracle, he thought deliriously, in which everyone shed their everyday fears and partook of some transcendental epiphany. 'We're all equals. The raw material of messianism. Leave your son here — we'll all learn with him,' he'd hear, happy. He imagined life in a time of war, say, when everything was totally destroyed and people were way too close to the limit to think about limits. 'Yes, give us your hand.' (But even in war, he counter-argued, on the other side was the Enemy.) I'm not being rational, he thought, on his way home, his son in tow. I've just pretended there was no problem, complacently putting things off, as always, mimicking the country I live in — this was inevitable. Why the hell is anyone obliged to look after my son? The government, he thought suddenly, remembering his political-candidate friend from years earlier, the gravity with which he'd raised his head to remember their little everyday Leviathan — the government was responsible.

On the street corner, his son wanted popcorn, but he refused him curtly, pulling him along by the hand, as it was almost lunchtime. The boy obeyed immediately. The government, he thought. His son was only alive because of the government, which was an abstract monster — left to a tribe or nature, he would have been dead in three days, useless. Which was what he, the father, had wished for, in a fit and a time that now seemed so long ago. On the next corner, a dark-skinned child without a shirt, of Felipe's age, was begging for money. His son held out his hand, smiling, to greet the boy, who didn't run away this time, but stared, intrigued at the smiling creature who looked like a little Chinaman. The father mechanically gave the child a coin (so his filthy hand wouldn't touch his son's open hand), which he took quickly and happily.

'Thanks, mister!' he said, and ran off to give it to an attentive adult who controlled the begging on the street from the shadows.

The government is selective, he thought. From where he was, it was comfortable not to like the government. And he was ungrateful — after all, the government tried everything it could to protect him from those other children, who lived in a different republic. But the irony (he immediately imagined a piece on the subject that he would never write) was lost half-a-dozen steps later; he had to think again about the son he was leading by the hand, in this new disruption. Maybe I haven't done everything I could have, he blamed himself. Maybe they (and now he included his wife) had abandoned the special training too soon — they'd only done two years intensively. Maybe they'd resigned themselves to too little. Maybe (now focused on himself again) he'd put his childish obsession with his own work, the brutal insecurity of those who write, over his own son. And he had, he mused — if his house were on fire, would he save his son or his manuscript? It was Sophie's choice revisited, and he smiled, his thoughts scattered; anything to avoid thinking about what he was leading by the hand. I can't be destroyed by literature, nor can I be destroyed by my son. I have a limit: I can only do what I can and know how to do, to the best of my abilities. Without thinking, he picked up the boy, who slumped deliciously over him, arms around his neck, and they climbed the stairs to the front door.

He only discovered how attached he was to his son the day that Felipe disappeared for the first time. It was, perhaps, he reflected soon afterwards, still in panic, unleashing his rare vocation for melodrama — which had now taken full control of him, the worst imaginable feeling in life — almost as terrible as the moment in which his son had revealed himself to the world, a feeling from which he would never completely recover, he told himself now in the mirror, of similar intensity, but it no longer had to do with chance. This time he had no excuse: he was responsible for his son. And he had to fill the gaping hole that grew bigger with each passing second with something, anything — but we're never prepared for the hole. His feeling of desperation wasn't sudden; it never is. It wasn't a cave-in; rather, the end of a mental climb that burned the cartridges of reason one by one until it seemed he had none left, and then the idea of solitude lost the comfortable charm of an idea and occupied his entire soul, where there was room for nothing else, except perhaps the thing-in-itself that he seemed to be looking so hard for: a feeling of abyss. (Don't move, because it hurts.)

This was what he calmly thought in retrospect almost twenty years later. At the time, everything was absurdly banal, and a first mechanical look around (where's Felipe?) was soon lost in other chores until it returned to the point (he was here, watching TV): the apartment wasn't so big that a child could hide in it, which he had never done, incidentally. The TV, which he checked like a Sherlock looking for clues (and the clues were there, but he didn't realise it), was showing the strange Japanese heroes drawn in primitive, aggressive lines that the father (brought up on Walt Disney) loathed but which his son was crazy about; such that, trisomic, he was able to understand that whole complex mythological hierarchy of beings (replicated in albums, magazines, collectors' stamps, dolls, videos, raffles, t-shirts, CDs, drawing books), repeat their names (which the father couldn't understand — the characters' names were already weird and then there was his son's painfully delayed linguistic development), utter their war cries, and endlessly act out that universal theogony on the living-room sofa, with colourful dolls that walked, talked, fought, lived, and died for hours and hours and hours on end in his son's hand, to an incomprehensible soundtrack — his son's voice reproducing bombs, explosions, arguments (changing his tone of voice with each change of character), barked commands, immediate responses, dreadful fights, and terrible deaths. All incomprehensible.

Only his sister seemed to understand what he was saying. Busy with other things, she was always listening attentively — and frequently staged her own little plays, as actress and director, unwittingly reproducing her own life, theatre and life being the same thing and, in a way, bringing her brother into reality. Docile, he always willingly accepted the roles she gave him, which were always himself, and was incredibly patient with his sister's occasional impatience. 'You stay here! Don't go anywhere! I'm your mother! That's it, just like that! Very good!' Because the father never spoke to anyone about his son's problem, she too, when she started school, never mentioned her brother's oddness to anyone; years later, her teacher would remember this strategic silence, a faithful reproduction of her father's silence. It was as if upbringing were an unconscious process — the most important things took place in darkness, more in the silent teachings of gesture, omission, and atmosphere than in edifying, logical, direct speech.

The door was open, the father realised — his son had gone out and left a sliver of a clue. He had no doubt taken the lift down nineteen floors, which he knew how to do. No, the doorman hadn't seen him, which didn't mean much — all he had to do was nip down to the garage for two minutes, there and back, and the boy could pass through the foyer without being noticed. A sign of the times, the building still didn't have the tall pointy-topped fences, security cameras, and electrical wires that would soon enclose the generous patio, open on all sides. It was fifteen metres from the foyer to the front pavement, where the father stationed himself, pathetic, looking from side to side, the whole world before him. He chose the path his son knew best, towards the centre of town, where he must have headed. Small hopes formed side by side with enormous fears. Maybe when I turn the corner he'll be there. The father needed to ask people if they'd seen him, but he felt an absurd inhibition, a kind of shame, for himself and his son, which made him seize up — or the simple male shame of asking for help, like in jokes about the differences between men and women. Men never ask for help, and he seemed to correspond to the cliché. A topographical cretin, the father was capable of driving around a neighbourhood ten times, lost, before asking someone how to get to the street he was looking for. But now it wasn't a street, it was a son. He'd have to find the right word to explain, since people didn't know. Perhaps he could say, 'Have you seen my son? He's got a problem,' or 'He's a little simple,' or 'He's mentally retarded,' and none of it corresponded either to his son or to what he wanted to say to define him. 'He's an affectionate child but a bit dopey.' Maybe it would be better like that. He couldn't say 'mongoloid', which hurt, or 'Down syndrome'. No one knew what that was in the 1980s.

'But who would kidnap my son?' was the only question he asked himself, gripped by a panic that grew with each block on which he didn't find him. A child had recently been kidnapped and murdered on the coast in a black-magic ritual — middle-class people, well fed, schooled, without the slightest social excuse, and the father even forgot his son momentarily to reflect on the inexplicable. God certainly wasn't a variable to consider in the scheme of things, but the Devil was vividly present in people's lives, he thought, taking refuge in abstraction (and the same logic that had killed the child), and he got goose bumps. Forget evil, he thought. Focus on the now, this precise moment, time slipping past in silence, and come back to your son. It was a calm Sunday morning. Thank goodness — fewer chances of his getting hit by a car. Felipe had trouble crossing streets due to his short-sightedness, typical of the syndrome. He also wasn't very autonomous; when he went to the bathroom, he frequently called out to his mother to help him wipe himself, and she, with infinite patience, slowly taught him the care and skill that would be his autonomy years later, but for now they were still in training. Scatological beings relieving themselves of waste daily, in programmed rituals, machines that required endless washing. For us, Alpha Pluses, with the intelligence of the Admirable New World, it seems easy.

The father quickened his step. In no time, he was running through the adjacent blocks — nothing, practically no one in the streets. His son could be anywhere. He might have found an open door, any one of the millions that exist in the world, and walked through it, climbed stairs, taken lifts; and if anyone found him they wouldn't know what to do, nor would he know how to explain who he was. Especially if even his own father didn't know who he was, thought the father, looking for an escape in his empty word-play. He went to the newsstand where he always took his son to buy magazines, and finally asked if anyone had seen him. It was easier there because they already knew him — he didn't have to explain anything. No, no one had seen the boy there. He left his phone number. 'If you do see him, please call.' He went in a circle around their building, moving through the streets. Nothing.

What talent did his son have, besides being an affectionate child, with fits of stubbornness? None, he concluded. All attempts to teach him to read and write had failed. Maybe it was too early: he was nine. Maybe it wasn't limited intelligence — that is, the inability to recognise a written sign as the representation of a sound (which was difficult) or an idea (easier, and which he did erratically, but not in the abstraction of letters; the first word he ever read was *Coca-Cola*). The question, mused the father, losing heart as he walked along, sinking into the paralysis of panic (where the hell had the bloody kid got to?), was that his grasp of language wasn't sophisticated enough for reading and writing to make sense; he had no syntax, verb tenses, plurals, or gender — nothing. All he knew were a few separate words, or blocks of two or three words. It wasn't enough, he thought, to catch a bus. But he doesn't have the maturity to catch a bus alone; he lives in a world of fantasy. What would he do if he saw this blue sign, the father wondered, again on the street corner near his building — Rua Dr Faivre? What would that mean to him? Nothing. Perhaps an indication of the way to his heroes' planet — and Felipe would say, arm extended, 'This way!' repeating some catchphrase from Pokémon, like a cartoon character, not a person.

He needed (and his panic increased) to call the police. I'm not going to manage on my own — and in five seconds flat foresaw a crazy sequence of searches that would culminate in a television interview, news stories, posters all over town, a collective commotion around his son. A cold chill ran down his spine, and he felt even more his definitive loss of freedom as someone marked until the end of time as the father who had lost his son — who, naturally, would never be found. He returned home in a sweat, from running around and the terror of the moment: with each second, the idea of his son's disappearance grew more and more concrete. He needed to readapt his soul to the new situation — absence. Talent. Yes, his son drew, he remembered, and it was as if it had redeemed him. Look: my son has qualities! Yes, he could draw, and he seemed quite original — although he didn't know it. He still had no notion of 'authorship', the primary — and granitic — pride of all art created in the last five hundred years. For the boy, the world had no hierarchy whatsoever in form or value — everything was of the same instantaneous essence at every instant. The father dragged himself home, in a fit of desolation. That which never was couldn't ever have been: that's how things worked. Deal with it, he repeated three or four times in his old game to test whether the meaning crumbled or held firm. He dealt with it.

There was the shock of leaving the school for normal children for his first special school, when the headmistress returned his son to him, essentially saying: We don't want your son — there are special schools for him, which are trained and equipped to help him. We're not. For the father, taking him to the special school was reliving that room at the clinic in Rio, when he realised for the first time that his world of references would always be definitively other. The boy had also felt the difference — in his first few months of special school, his reaction had been withdrawal and silence. He didn't recognise himself in the others around him. For a while, he would still find it relatively hard to be around his peers, that disparate set of cases at once similar and very different that shared his school with him.

The father began to realise that special children were much more radically different from one another than children in the normal world. The overwhelming stimuli they received (they heard the word 'no' thousands of times more than any normal person), the endless differences in their neurological receptors, and their lack of normal references — all this contributed to a special kind of solitude, at once abundant, emotive, and buoyant, which sometimes exploded in deaf aggression. In his case, it was as if the desperate need for normality that haunted the father had been passed down to his son, whose only beacons were his father's, not his own, ever. As if his son had no yardstick of his own; as if he didn't have the mind to create one, which was absurd.

For his son, perhaps, it was truly unbearable to recognise in those children who barely knew how to speak, in those beings with no motor skills — who dragged legs, gaped, screeched for no reason, and had fits of unrelenting stubbornness or total alienation. Perhaps it was truly unbearable to see them as his own group, his peers, his tribe — as if he had also absorbed his father's resistance to the rest of the world, reproducing, in his every breath, every detail of his father's sentiments. Many of the unpleasant features that he recognised in the others were also his own, after all. It was as if, at the special school he'd begun to attend, Felipe was finally seeing himself in his own dimension, and it hurt. The horror of the mirror — the inability to see how similar we are to others (although, thought the father, one would have to establish separate groups for similar cases, which special schools tried to do, but the groups formed would never have the homogeneity of the standard of reference). Little by little, the isolation of the first few months melted away and, stimulated by the pedagogical infrastructure and an excellent teacher, his son started drawing more and in a more disciplined way.

School created a parameter: the father saw himself as a boy again, remembering how frustrated he'd felt when he read about the school of his dreams in England, where everyone could do whatever they wanted — a teenager's paradise. He remembered he'd stolen the book *Summerhill* from a bookshop. He read it avidly in two days, a little Rousseau rediscovering the delights of natural freedom. 'Why wasn't I schooled like that?' he had wondered, trying to sustain a set of self-schooling principles of his own account, in the confusion of being sixteen, lighting a cigarette and blowing out the smoke like the adults he saw in real life and the cinema. He developed two dogmas of youth: first, freedom is an absolute value; second, evil is an illness, not a choice. Nothing new: he'd fully assimilated the best his time had to offer, which wasn't much. It was only years later, through literature, that he finally began to escape totalising abstractions. It was important to focus, always, on the here-and-now, that infinite web of complications that ties us down, and only then could the rest make a difference.

Here and now: returning home without his son, the same son he'd wished dead the minute he was born, and who now, with his absence, seemed to be killing him.

Their only option was to call the police. No one had seen the boy anywhere. He should start with the phone book, he imagined. An inept man; whenever he had to come out of his shell for anything outside of himself, he got caught up in an interminable mental film in which he wasn't sure if he was the director or protagonist, or perhaps a deaf marionette. He called a few numbers, but no one answered on that Sunday morning — he'd probably dialled them wrongly, he thought, growing irritated. A mountain of complications seemed to be piling up by the second: he had to do something. He picked a nearby address (the juvenile police station, or something like that — it was a long name) and decided to go there by car, happy because he knew what to do, to get someone physically in front of him who could point him in the right direction.

It was his resistance to the police that bothered him, the idea that he'd have to place his delicate little foot out in the real world, in that other parallel republic that he pretended didn't exist except as newspaper stories, statistics, or the focus of moral indignation from time to time. The police: people who were always trying to control others, in keeping with the law. When he watched police films on TV, he even fancied he could be a police officer (he had recurrent dreams of changing jobs, imagining himself doing completely different things from those he did. 'How would I feel in this job?' he asked himself. He imagined what his friends would say, seeing him in uniform, hat, and badge: 'Now you've really entered the system! The university was just an appetiser!'). He could be a policeman, he smiled. Not on the beat, as he was essentially a watchmaker, but in an office somewhere, dealing with statistics, perhaps. Or drawing up plans to fight crime. We need to get our men over to this neighbourhood, which has a 57.2 per cent higher homicide rate than the rest of the city. 'Let's go, boys!' But when he took his eyes off the TV, the image grew dull, hazy, and he could no longer tell things apart — crime and the police, the police and crime — because Brazil's history didn't help much, and the dictatorship had scrambled the deck even further. When the state has a not-so-secret vocation for crime, the people get lost, and then it really does become a free-for-all. The doors to the economy had been flung open, but none of the major political projects of the twentieth century had helped separate right from wrong; nor did the fact that so many Brazilians lived by their wits help matters any. Even he, an educated citizen, often got mixed up about what he could and couldn't do; he always had a good justification up his sleeve if anyone were to ask but, like everyone else, he kept quiet. Nothing to declare, he was sad to remember a minister of justice saying. Nothing to declare.§§ We have nothing to declare. Fuck them all, I'm looking after my own skin.

Now he found himself in front of a closed police station. There must have been a mistake. It had been shut down, he realised, seeing the broken windows, graffiti on the walls, a bum sleeping in the shade of the building. Why didn't I call first? There was an

---

§§ Brazil's long-serving government minister Armando Falcão used this expression whenever he was pressured by journalists, especially after controversial government decisions.

abandoned car with its tires missing in the haunted parking lot. He felt the strangeness of that Sunday morning, its sharp feeling of incompetence, himself a Kafka character. 'Don't you want to find your son?' the stage director asked him. He remembered the Stanislavski exercise from his acting days, the realistic scene and the false scene: the actress looking for the needle she had lost, wailing melodramatically. 'Well,' said the director, 'if you *really* don't find the needle, you're fired.' And she started looking for it in tense silence, inch by inch, the drama contained, but *true*, to everyone's relief. True feeling, he mused again: one needed an entire cosmogony in order to believe in it. And I'm always having to watch my step, he would have said if anyone had asked.

Paralysed in the empty parking lot, he remembered his only encounter with the police, in 1972, in the São Paulo neighbourhood of Vila Mariana. The world was so small that he was actually able to drive in São Paulo; he was the theatre group's driver, using an old two-carburettor Variant to transport pieces of scenery and actors and actresses here and there, all staying with different friends and relatives. Late one night, he took some members of the group — three actors and two actresses — back to the borrowed basement where they were staying, in an old house. The owner and friend (who was away) lived in a cottage out back and let them stay in the comfortable basement of the house in front, which he had rented out to a couple for decades. The actors and actresses had invited him in for a coffee: a typical troupe of the 1970s, long hair, sandals, beards, guitar, backpacks, marijuana, bell-bottoms, peace, and love. They laughed as they walked down the side of the house and found the door to the basement, which had a separate entrance, closed with a padlock. What was that all about? When they turned around, they made out a figure darting back to the house, through the front door.

Intrigued, he noticed the light on and, although it was late, climbed the porch steps and knocked on the door — and after an indecisive silence, without opening the door, a frightened woman's voice said, 'My husband's called the police! Go away!'

Even worse: he discovered that the man — the figure they had seen — had also locked the high front gate with a padlock as soon as they had walked through it. They were trapped in a cage, he quickly deduced. He was the only one there who knew of the long-standing feud between the landlord and the renters, who (of course, the penny suddenly dropped!) must have thought the bunch of pot-smokers was there to make their lives hell rather than spend four innocent days putting on a play. 'I need to make a phone call!' he said, and jumped up to climb the two-or-three-metre gate. As his feet hit the pavement, he heard the sudden braking of a police van, and (in a moment of terror) saw a police officer approach, yelling, and pointing what looked like a machine gun at him. Like in the movies, he put his hands in the air and immediately started explaining, but nobody listened. He was frisked and roughed up, then dragged to the van and thrown in the back, the door slamming shut behind him. As he tried to get up in the dark, he banged his head on the low roof; it hurt dreadfully. The only person capable of explaining what was going on (him, the troupe's driver) was now in the back of the van. There was a big, chaotic discussion on the pavement: thank goodness they were talking. He started shouting through the air vents, trying to explain. Suddenly, the van was opened again for another member of the group, then another and another, tossed in like packages. He heard only one voice, repeating, 'You can explain down at the station!' He worried about the women, but they had special privileges and were put in the front of the van. He whispered his biggest fear to his pals. 'Is the pot in your bags?'

No, they'd thrown it out. He sighed with relief, closed his eyes in the dark, and thought: Yes, we can explain. We're actors, not criminals.

Now, gazing at the empty parking lot, he felt terror creeping up on him again. If that had happened today, he probably would have been gunned down jumping over the gate before he'd even had a chance to open his mouth, he thought, exaggerating as usual, and everyone would think it fair and good. What was he doing jumping over the gate? One less thief. Now it was his son on the line: one less. Subtraction was the rule. Back home, he and his wife were overwhelmed with a paralysing fatalism. They managed to talk to someone on the phone, a polite but bureaucratic voice that said something like, 'Wait twenty-four hours' and gave him a few other snippets of legal advice to which he was unable to pay attention. He felt a kind of resistance to reality: his son's disappearance didn't make any sense, therefore he hadn't disappeared.

But while he roamed the streets searching for his son, and his wife knocked on doors in the building looking for news of his whereabouts (maybe the boy was right there, in someone else's flat?), a miraculous phone call from a neighbour brought the episode to an end. Two military police officers had found Felipe in the nearby university parking lot, playing in a jeep with its top down, excitedly chattering to himself at the steering wheel, living out his autistic pantomime. They had realised, naturally, that he was a child with problems — and had noticed there was no one around to keep an eye on him. Before they'd even had a chance to call in the incident, a neighbour had happened past, recognised the boy, given them his address, and called the family. The father had been past there twice, but some stupid block had stopped him remembering to check the inside parking lot, perhaps afraid (exaggerating again) that someone he knew, maybe a student, might recognise him and he'd have to open up.

Opening up: at the Vila Mariana police station, as he was escorted with the troupe to the district chief's office, actually a large hall — a patio of miracles filled with beggars, miscreants, loafers, bored officers, the occasional scream, figures from another world of the parallel republic that he'd never seen so close (and the country was still, in 1972, living the innocence of its crimes) — he tried to simulate importance, boost his own morale (someone who'd read Nietzsche; someone who'd finished high school; someone who knew how to fix watches; someone who was definitely going to be a writer; someone who, judging from his posture, or even his fair hair, German, Polish, or Italian looking, his glasses included in the socio-racial-economic package, had been raised to live on the upper floor; someone who had a literary understanding of life and dreamed of a universal humanism; a man of letters — all said and done, a statistical rarity). He lit a cigarette with the studied gesture of an actor in front of the district chief's desk. Like in *The Threepenny Opera*, he was momentarily the leader of a small band of criminals — one black, one with long hair, one half-Indian, half-black, two sloppily dressed brunettes, practically women of the night, poor, all skinny, ridiculous aspiring actors and actresses seeking respectability who, petulantly, worked their feet through the crack in the door of humanity to push their way in. But he didn't have time to expound on the group's qualities: the district chief's hand flew up one millimetre from his face, making the cigarette disappear.

'No one smokes in here!' And to the officer who had escorted him, he asked, 'Who are they?'

'That complaint about the squatters.'

Sitting on a bench, a filthy beggar covered in ulcers pointed at one of the actors, with Jesus Christ hair down to his shoulders, and let out a toothless cackle that turned into a hoarse cough.

'Check out the hair!'

Out of the blue, a gentleman appeared in a suit and tie, the respectable house owner who had called the police, and the scene acquired the tone of a vaudeville comedy.

'They're all squatting in my house. I locked the basement to be safe. I don't want them there,' said the man in the suit.

'Are you the owner?' asked the district chief.

'Yes,' he lied.

The district chief (thirty years of jail and bail) ran his irritated eyes over the sorry lot in front of him, all kids, and in one second took in the subtle nuances that distinguished burglars and murderers from crazy kids on a weekend frolic. He may have been wondering if there was a son or daughter of someone important among them. He made his decision suddenly, already thinking about something else.

'They can get out of the house and find some place else to stay.'

A repeated hand gesture revealed his boredom (go on, beat it!), and he sat down again.

The aspiring writer wasn't satisfied. He saw a crumpled copy of the newspaper O Estado de São Paulo on the man's desk and, in a flash, thought he'd found salvation.

'We're actors, not bums,' he said dramatically. 'We've been staging a play at the Paulo Eiró Theatre for the last three days. Directed by W. Rio Apa. Here it is.' He quickly opened the newspaper with shaking hands, found the cultural pages, and held up the discreet article in the corner of a page. He insisted, pointing aggressively at the owner now. 'How is it that he only realised today that his house had been invaded? The real owner of the house lent us the basement.' It was hard to explain. He found it difficult to spell out the details, and the district chief, after quickly assessing the importance of the article (which was zero), gave him a look bordering on fury, that said: What does this kid want? I'm giving him a chance to walk out of here.

'Have you got the rental contract?' asked the district chief. 'A document to prove the loan? Do you?'

Silence. The man turned to the police officer, his arm shaking in the same irritated gesture.

'Take this lot back and have them vacate the place. Now get out of here because I've got more important things to do.'

The future writer tried to contest Solomon's verdict, taking the complaint to the highest appeal, but the officer (a large man who proved surprisingly kind) gently pulled him out of there with the rest of the group, almost like a friend showing his buddies around or taking them for a beer, practically hugging them as he walked. He whispered, 'C'mon folks, before he blows his top. Now everyone can ride in the front of the van! You're my guests.'

The police escort to evict them — a driver and an armed officer — went in another car, a vee-dub. At one point, the policeman turned to the black member of the group, in the back seat.

'Tell me, nigga (by which he meant: *Look, I'm calling you nigga, but you can call me whitey — to me, all Brazilians are equal*) ... Tell me, you must have a bit of a smoke every now and then, right? I know you theatre folk.' His laugh was long and understanding. 'Once we picked up some big-shot TV actors, man!' The policeman's arms steered the car around Vila Mariana's dark street corners, while he chatted as if he were at a bar. 'Dude, you should've seen the amount of weed they had!' He laughed disarmingly again.

'None of us are into that,' came an unsure voice from the back seat, not believing what it was saying. The fright of their absurd arrest slowly started to fade, although a slight tremor escaped and lodged in their bodies. And the aspiring writer wondered what to do with the troupe, in São Paulo, out on the street after midnight, that raggedy bunch, and laughed nervously. Redistribute them around town.

'You guys were lucky,' said the policeman, slowing down to point over their heads at a building, the headquarters of the notorious political police agency Doi-Codi, yet another of the country's parallel republics. 'Even generals' sons get it in there. They can get rough.'

It was an eviction of backpacks, tracksuits, pillows, blankets, and a guitar, all stuffed into the back of the Variant. He phoned his guru, who gave him instructions to take them all to where he was staying — a small flat, where they'd camp temporarily. On the pavement, a short, pot-bellied police officer, also friendly (a caricature, with a cigarette dangling from his lips), machine gun slung over his shoulder, looked on in sincere surprise at the two girls carrying the last pillows to the car. He whispered to one of them, his concern legitimate, 'Did your mother let you join a theatre group?'

Fifteen years later, the writer took the lift downstairs to the pavement in front of his building to wait for the police car to bring his missing Felipe back. The car pulled up with its lights flashing silently and the boy got out, smiling and happy for having been escorted back in a *real* (a word he'd learned and repeated a lot) police car, absolutely oblivious to the gravity of what had happened. He was holding a yellow plastic sword and wearing a black Batman's cape, a Superman t-shirt, a colourful hat, purple shorts, and a pair of sandals — a happy little scarecrow. He pointed his sword at the top of the car.

'Look!' he said, calling his father by his first name. 'See! Real lights!'

A subtle shadow of mistrust passed through one of the young officer's eyes.

'Are you really his dad?'

The boy had never called him Dad and never would — only by his first name. And for an absurd second he almost found himself having to prove who he was, a respectable man, and not a kidnapper of lost children. At that same instant, his wife hugged the child and cried, 'Son, you can't just run off like that, or the police'll get you!' Which the father immediately tried to fix. 'Just as well the police found you, Felipe!' he said, acting out the cartoon pantomime that he always did with his son. 'You were saved by the forces of good! Right?'

His son joined in, raised his sword, and repeated an incomprehensible command from his Japanese cartoons. It wasn't the right time to try to make him understand what had happened and to tell him for the thousandth time that he shouldn't go anywhere alone or without talking to his parents first. Now they needed to prove that they were his parents, but it was no longer necessary — the effusive reunion was a clear demonstration of their affection. And the boy used the magic word when he hugged his mother: *Mumsy!* When they'd finished hugging, the officers gave them a detailed account of how they'd found Felipe. The father thanked them, moved, and handed one of them some money that he'd taken out of his wallet before coming down. 'This,' he tried to explain almost without looking them in the eye, 'is just a little something to help out and thank you for your work.' One of the officers said discreetly, 'Please, that's not necessary, we're only doing our job.' But he insisted, 'Please, take it, it's the least I can do — we were getting desperate and didn't know what to do.' They looked at one another for a second, as if in an urgent assembly, and accepted the money. Before leaving, they took down some details, such as names — for the police report, they said.

As they went upstairs, the father felt a pang in his heart: What would you say if a student offered you money because your class was good? Do you see the dimension of what you've done? Is your humanity any different from theirs? Every case is different, he tried to counter-argue. Things are never absolute: in life there are no qualitative differences between our deeds; only quantitative, and these are what matter. Those young men are no older than twenty-five or twenty-six, he thought, standing in front of the lift, forgetting to open the door. It's always a ... A what? You've simply opened another door to corruption. Don't complain a few years from now when they come to collect. That's culture. Just as much as your Nietzsche. And in this area, you're stronger. Brazil isn't Sweden, he argued, ashamed. And at this rate, he counter-argued, it never will be. But they found my son. Yes, it's true. But this is a syndrome (he opened the door now, relieved): you have a guilt complex, a disorder brought on by a heavy soul. He imagined that the lift might not budge with the weight of his guilt complex, and smiled at the simple humour of the idea. The door finally closed and the lift moved.

Years went by.

The father felt as if he'd entered another limbo, in which time, passing, was always in the same place — a calm stability, one of the small utopias that, with a little luck, everyone experiences at some stage in life. The wonderful power of routine, he thought ironically. It makes everything into the same thing, and that is exactly what we want. But there was a reason: his son wasn't ageing. And besides his mind, which was always the same, the unfathomable mysteries of genetics had caused him to grow only a little, in a slight case of dwarfism. A Peter Pan, he lived each day exactly like the last — and the next. Incapable of entering the abstract world of time, the idea of past and future never took root in his cheerful head; each morning, without realising it, he lived the dream of eternal return. The seven days of the week (which his parents tried to explain to him thousands of times) were an incomprehensible set of logarithms, a jumble of references of impenetrable complexity. Sundays and Wednesdays, Saturdays and Tuesdays and Fridays and every other day had a similar, idyllic morning: the world began again. It was useless drawing up calendars, marking each day with an X, patiently explaining daily tasks according to the time machine that the division of the week represented. At any moment he would go over to the board and draw an X, proud of a task he'd completed, or a series of colourful signs in that row of inviting little boxes, until he heard a dismayed 'no', which caused him to ignore the calendar from that point on for fear of making a mistake. He despised time, because he didn't understand it. In fact, he ignored the things he didn't understand. He went around them, didn't see them, forgot them, erased them, or used pantomime to make what was otherwise meaningless physically palpable — like laughing at an incomprehensible joke in a group of adults, imitating their grimaces and shaking heads. He was an involuntary parody of a tiny adult, and somehow disarmed everyone — transformed into pure gesture, hollow bones. As for time, the following month another calendar would go up on the wall; more patent, detailed explanations: today is Wednesday; today you have your swimming lesson. Have you got your backpack ready? Which he did with great care and attention — and slowly. But he was proud of the task completed: 'Look! See!' And he'd do his champion's pose with each bed made, a hero's achievement.

The flat was his territory, which he only left (and only wanted to leave), sometimes against his will, for specific, planned tasks at different times of day and stages in life: school, swimming lessons, walks, music lessons. He would never have the autonomy to go out alone. Yes, he could be trained to do so, if there was a systematic effort (which there wasn't), but the world outside was becoming too frightening. His disappearance that Sunday morning had just been a sample. (There was another occasion, on a weekend at the beach; he had simply started walking, a determined athlete working out, following the bay towards the next beach, until after two hours of desperation another police car found him and brought him back. This time, the remorseful father didn't corrupt anyone — he sent a fax to their superior, lavishing well-deserved praise on the officers responsible and citing their names.) There are children with Down syndrome who develop good autonomy in this sense, but Felipe never did. The odyssey of going to the corner to buy a newspaper, for example, was intersected by thousands of inviting stimuli that couldn't be controlled within a mission with a set time-frame — walking to the newsstand, buying the newspaper, waiting for the change, and returning home. He would also have to confront a world that was unprepared for him and, at times, aggressive. Once some neighbouring kids, with the measured cruelty of someone playing a joke on the classic village idiot, put him in the lift, pressed the button for the top floor, turned out the light, and closed the door, leaving him alone. His terror of the dark — perhaps the memory of the carousel of stimuli to which he had been subjected in his first few months of life — came flooding back.

Music lessons. For a time, they tested his musical abilities, in keeping with the myth that Down children had a special sensibility for music. To compensate for the problem (the father thought, always trying to go against the flow, like a right-handed person who insists on writing with his left hand), special magical territories were created in which Down children, as in certain medieval beliefs about madmen and prodigies, saw, felt, and experienced what others didn't see, feel, or experience, which was true to the same degree that the differential exists for everyone — that is, we are unique beings, for better or for worse. They were polite ways of dealing with the difference. He once heard a stranger say that children 'like his son' were highly intelligent, and perceived things that others couldn't. The man actually lowered his voice, as if confiding a rare secret. A friend, years earlier, had told him that the child's pure state of emotion gave him a superior understanding of life and the world. His emotion was his understanding — and now the idea found resonance in the father's head. There was some truth to it. The world of emotion is this child's talent, he thought, trying to formulate a description. Yes, as was the case with everyone; but with Down children, and special children in general, the simplest emotions were the only areas of meaning in life that didn't appear to suffer any handicaps. Yes, emotion was a kind of understanding for these children, the father mused, the only path to understanding and communication. Felipe hugged as if surrendering himself to the world with abandon. He was as free in his affections as a dog lolling happily in the sun on a veranda — almost as if his hugs weren't gestures born of human culture, but pure, natural impulse.

Music, on the other hand, was the enactment of music. It was sitting at the piano at music school simulating a concert — every gesture studied, except for the notes and their brutal demands. And zero concentration — just the teacher's patience, which was enormous. Those simple pairs of notes, tiny coordinated gestures, easy melodies, just a scale of different sounds to start with, turned into a horrendous sweatshop of meaningless sequences. Felipe suffered; his hands didn't obey his soul, which didn't hear the sound, which was on another frequency. As if his perception couldn't distinguish sound from gesture, everything was an interminable, delicious cartoon that he mimicked. There was no place in him for that kind of discipline. The thought of having to go to music lessons twice a week induced panic and some of the few lies he ever told. 'I've got a headache,' he'd say, a melodramatic hand pressed to his forehead, overacting the part, which he took very seriously. 'It's terrible.' He'd squeeze his eyes shut in the enormous falseness of his pain. His parents finally gave up, to everyone's relief.

His talent for buffoonery didn't go to waste, however, and

came to good use on the stage. At the special school he attended daily, a patient and talented art teacher put on surprising theatrical numbers with that disparate group of children. One such number was a simplified version of *The Comedy of Errors*. The concept was original: on stage, the children lip-synced their own voices, previously recorded in isolated passages that were later strung together into a sequence. As such, each individual line, painstakingly practised by the children before they were recorded, served as the backdrop for a delicious, ingenuous pantomime, which they acted out with touching dedication and efficiency. They would never have been able to memorise the longer lines — and some of them, like his son, would never naturally produce a complete sentence with a relative clause followed by a coordinate clause. (The only structure he managed on a day-to-day basis was a basic subject-predicate construction, in that order, and never in the passive voice.)

But with the recording done in parts, the story got told, and beautifully — the skit was delightful from beginning to end, and part of its beauty was the careful, imaginary declaiming of the children's lines. They acted on stage at the limits of their fragility and responsibility, delicately balanced dancers advancing as a group, one foot at a time on the tightrope of performance, watching over and helping one another. The father was pretty sure his son didn't understand the play, except in his own isolated gags, but it didn't matter: it was a pleasurable task with a beginning, a middle, and an end, which he carried out with a complete sense of duty. He had learned (and understood) that everything should be well done, and threw himself into the task at hand.

At the end of the day, the pleasure was narcissistic, a streak that was growing more accentuated in the child. While in his early years it had been a mere case of childish self-centeredness during a phase in which he was undeniably the centre of the universe, slowly polished over the years until he became aware of others' rights, now the pleasure was narcissistic, unfettered by censorship — exhibitionism in its crude state, which his father had also tried to polish, though without much success. Because audiences are always prepared to forgive prodigies, he felt the stage was his party: at the end, during the applause, he wanted to show off more, and came downstage to clown around and demand more applause, until someone yanked him away like in an involuntary Jerry Lewis comedy or like Peter Sellers refusing to die in the first scene of *The Party*.

In another number, formally dressed in a simulacrum of a tuxedo, the boy dubbed a fat opera singer in histrionic gestures, a feat he would later repeat at home for the relatives, and would try to repeat several times a day to whomever would listen until his father made him stop or he became absorbed in another activity. Some time later, with a home video camera, the father recorded some short gags and simple magic tricks with his son — it was entertaining. He created a frame for Felipe that gave him a purpose, polishing his gestures and excesses until the boy saw himself (which he did a thousand times over) on the television and computer as an artist. Education by fine-tuning — as if the director's hand explained: 'Look, like this, repeating the gesture once only, it's even funnier.' His assimilation of actions was instantaneous, well before their meanings. He liked to put on a pair of sunglasses, sit in a folding chair, and shout: 'Camera! Action!' Life was a cartoon: he tested gestures on the tolerant audience of his family to see which ones got a laugh, then repeated them to exhaustion. He didn't have the slightest notion of artistic hierarchy, good or bad — for him, there was no difference between a gag repeated three times at the dinner table and an actor declaiming Shakespeare. Like an unconscious harbinger of the times, in his hands the whole spectacle of the world was devoid of seriousness. The father wondered what he saw when he saw himself in the recorded skits. To what extent did he perceive himself?

In one of the theatre group's plays in the 1970s, like the one they had staged in São Paulo, the father had played a beggar who had killed his mother and gone to confession at the Temple of Seven Confessions. Set in the Middle Ages, it had been a kind of stage-truth, developed in improvisations that were emotive and emotional, each actor creating much of his or her own lines until the final result was honed by a director with an iron fist. There was a little bit of everything in the conception of the production: shards of Jung and Freud, exercises in humiliation and letting go, overshadowed by a certain medieval Christianity impregnated with an inescapable lust for guilt. The rehearsals had been almost religious — at times, true acts of repentance. The director believed that concentration shouldn't be the mere expression of a technique, an exercise in self-control; rather, it should be fusion with a true inner voice. The utopia of 'true feelings' was in the air: everyone was seeking 'true emotions,' the primal scream, the supposedly raw, uncontrollable reality of archetypes, and in this search the line between the aesthetic world and the world of life wasn't clear. Catharsis was the key word: to cite Aristotle, the idea was to purge the emotions through a 'deep' (a key word in everything they did) experience of the tragedy of life. It was anti-Brecht: the dream of zero distance. Because there was never any intention of parody, and the acting itself was desperately trying to be the 'thing in itself', rather than a reading or interpretation of it, each gesture bordered insidiously on the ridiculous, its threatening double. But the ridiculous, here, wasn't just an expression of social shame, a comment from the outside, an exterior gaze, a 'petit bourgeois' sentiment (to use the jargon of the time). What threatened to explode the pathetically false shell of repentance was the destructive force of laughter against the empire, and pretension, of appearance. In short, the aestheticising of life was what was ridiculous about it — the shadow of kitsch, a parallel world, a phantom of our gestures, a prêt-à-porter frame to lend colour to the impossible insufficiency of life. Pretending that a gesture produced by the world of culture is natural, authentic, true; a transcendent, inevitable expression; and the fruit of nature rather than one possible choice among thousands of others, for which we are responsible, is also the essence of messianism. Messiahs, of any kind, are those who attribute a naturalness — if not divinity — that will never be attached to their own carefully studied gestures.

This was what he mulled over, years later, trying to understand, as he watched his son showing off so shamelessly at the front of the stage in *The Comedy of Errors* until an adult came and led him back behind the curtains. To Felipe, others were merely a source of imitation, never of interaction (except for his affections, when nature took over and imitation fell silent). His son sometimes had to be snapped out of his own private theatre (imaginary dialogues that he whispered between cartoon heroes with expressive tones, gestures, and dramatic pauses), as if his hypnotic alternative world had spirited him away. Too much TV, his father sometimes thought, looking for something to blame for that dialogue-for-one, but that wasn't it. Imaginary dialogue, an integral part of the linguistic acquisition of all children, had been a constant in Felipe's circular life — as if he was always practically the same age, with the same system of comprehension, reference, and language. It was a refuge with autistic features, albeit soft. He preferred this refuge, this immersion in his own stories, the repetition of his TV heroes and mythical figures, to contact with other children. It was a sign that time had finally passed and that he no longer wanted to be confused with a 'child'.

With some pride, he kept a very sparse beard, which he liked to tend in an exceedingly long ritual. He tried adult company with his parents, and parroted gestures, laughter, and attitudes, but the content was inaccessible to him — it was the theatrics that were important, feeling he was a member of an 'adult' community, for the emotional contact. Having guests over was invariably an event — a short, intense reception. When it was someone he knew, there were the typical phrases and gestures of camaraderie or good-humoured provocation; when it was someone he didn't know, an inquisitive, friendly 'Hi,' or even a disarming and hilarious 'Who are you?' The dialogues were short, with key questions and more-or-less standard answers, always with a big, sincere smile on his face — and off he'd go back to his life, in front of the TV or the computer.

The father tried to stay abreast of technological advances in order to stimulate his son, starting with TV from a young age. And, surreptitiously, his efforts exercised an inverse influence on him — a father also permanently unprepared for mature adult life of any kind, he thought with a smile. And it was possible that his daughter, who had nothing to do with it, suffered the consequences of having a father who refused to grow up. Years later, he imagined, it was easy to clearly map everything out, in possession of a good theory, but in real life we didn't have time to think about anything. The present was a kind of fumbling in the dark, he thought, justifying himself.

But there are objective criteria, he thought. The child needs to be constantly exposed to language. Television. A light bulb came on in his head: it was simple. Someone who had seen a black-and-white TV for the first time at the age of eight and who had spent his entire youth hating that box, hating soap operas, hating the news, and who was fully convinced that the all-powerful TV network Rede Globo was the mother of all the country's evil, a sinister figure making Brazil's then 90 million inhabitants an inert mass of stupid robots repeating everything they saw and heard, would now finally buy a television. It was total, pleasurable surrender, with the alibi that his son required stimulation. He wantonly plunged into the fascinating world of disposable images. First came the TV, then one of the first VCRs, a huge thing bought in thirty-six monthly instalments, so the children could watch stimulating cartoons repeated to exhaustion — that was his excuse.

It surprised him that the children always wanted to watch the same cartoons and hear the same stories over and over. His daughter knew all the stories by heart and repeated them for her brother, who was at once present and absent, and acted out familiar situations in which she was the mother and he was her son. Like children all over the world, imitation was the driving force behind everything that was created, thought the father, always insecure in his work at a writer. Fortunately, he lived light-years away from Brazil's literary world, deep in the dense silence of the province, which protected him, also autistic, from what he imagined to be a sad, distressing, aggressive mediocrity, against which he felt the stirring of a discreet resentment he needed to control, the fuel of everyone who produced art — that is, who produced that which, as a rule, was of no interest to anyone. Or at least the art I produce, literature, he conceded, while watching music videos on TV that were profoundly interesting, always, to millions of people.

He spent a few years (he blamed himself, still in the Temple of Seven Confessions) more concerned with himself than with his children, all that time writing and rewriting books that didn't exist, that didn't get published; or that, once published, didn't get read, and that at the end of the day didn't sell, in a powerful, asphyxiating non-existence. His books were different from one another, but he didn't seem to learn anything from the experience, moving in circles, himself an amplified expression of his son, always deep in his own labyrinth. Was it an artistic project or a therapeutic one, he sometimes asked himself, pen in hand, gazing at a blank page. Stubbornness: he was stubborn. He disguised his oversized pride of his imaginary qualities with the friendly manner of one who appeared to be like everyone else. He gradually began to see himself as the passive expression of an existential project that was elsewhere, designed by someone other than himself. Maybe I'm working in the service of something false, a secret glass diamond of which I am victim. Which wouldn't be (he admitted in surprise) a complete disaster. Through writing he might discover something, though, he quickly realised, without confusing life and literature, separate entities that should be kept at a respectful distance from one another. I'm only interesting if I write myself, which makes me vanish without a trace, he imagined with a smile, foreseeing a perfect crime. No one will ever know, he dreamed, hidden in some refuge of his childhood.

The empire of images: TV, videos, films, computer, cartoons and, last but not least, painting. Little by little, Felipe's unpretentious drawings, coloured pens on paper, began to attract attention. He produced cartoons, one sheet of paper after another, schematic lines making the frames of a mental story that he explained or reproduced as he went along, like a pictorial shorthand with a soundtrack: dramatic dialogues, mythical refrains, sometimes powerful bombs, an intense, solitary theatre completely isolated from the world, except for the evocation of what he saw in the colourful box of the TV — and his lines tried to accompany that journey. When a drawing was barely half done, he'd turn the page to start the next, such that the paper was never enough.

The father remembered how at the age of sixteen he had confessed to his guru that he didn't understand a thing about painting. His master had told him that painting was fundamental and that he should study it if he wanted to be a writer — advice he had immediately obeyed, starting with serial publications bought at newsstands, then the history of art, and finally outright imitation. He bought oil paints, canvases, and brushes, and started copying famous paintings; first a small Manet (his childish error had been to use oils when the original was in pastels), then a Munch, followed by Van Gogh, which he filled

191

with delightfully thick brush strokes. There was an illusion of science about it: he divided the canvas into squares with a pencil, then the painting to be copied, and struggled to maintain the logic of its proportions. He painted Gauguin on some double doors at the theatre group's headquarters, four paintings filling the sheets of chipboard. The copies were childish, really bad, but he realised the power of colour — all one had to do was combine them according to some mystery of composition (which was already there in the original, of course), and the effect was always good, as long as you didn't get too close. Colours aside, he developed a taste for everything that was pessimistic, heavy, and tragic: Munch and, above all, Ensor, those skulls dissolving into real, everyday nightmares. Where did he get that from — he who spent his life laughing? Every year he dreamed of going back to painting so he could play at copying, but he would never do it again until his last breath. Revisiting the past was never worth it, his childhood actor-friend used to say. When it happens, we are so needy that we are suffocated by our inability to immobilise time and life. What was sweet was over. *The End*, he read on his imaginary canvas. Don't insist.

Now he saw his son doing the same thing he used to do: copying, not paintings, but what appeared to be reality. The boy was keenly observant, but not of wholes or of proportions — his reality was distorted by a gaze incapable of creating hierarchical relationships or a more precise sense of proportion or perspective, which gave his lines their charm. The world was flat, and everything was up close. The size of things wasn't an abstract category — at the age of twenty-five, he still believed that there was more juice in the tall, thin glass than in the short, fat one with double the volume, or that ten toothpicks in a row spread out represented more than twenty toothpicks close to one another. Which didn't matter at all: if his father told him it wasn't true, he, oblivious to the fact, would press his hand to his forehead ruefully and say, 'Wrong again! By Jupiter!' or some other exclamation from his cartoons, like 'Miserable Rat!' from Captain Haddock — another of his passions, which always made him laugh. And his eyes would already be casting about for something more interesting to play with. All of his intelligence, mused his father, was in his perception of the value of social gestures, which he always tried to mimic. Who was the child who did those drawings?

The papers flew. Out of prudence, and a certain peasant notion that paper was a product comparable to gold or silver, to be treated with care and respect (to this day, he can't throw away a half-used piece of paper — he folds them in half, and makes notebooks out of the piles of blank scraps in his drawer with paper clips), the father started giving him used pages to draw on the back, among which were originals and typed copies of his already published novels, until his wife was called into the school for a meeting with the director. A classmate had taken one of Felipe's drawings home as a present, and on the back were racy passages from *Tentative Adventures*, indecorous swear words, and a sex scene. From then on, he carefully checked the pages he gave his son — not for his son's sake, as he couldn't read them, but for others. Maybe he shouldn't write that kind of scene any more, joked the father, half-serious. Someone had already told him, 'Such good books! So interesting! But the swear words ... What a shame! They spoil everything!'

Sex. Many years earlier, a colleague from the university had asked, over coffee, 'Forgive the question, but what about sex, for Felipe?' The boy was four or five at the time, and the father hadn't thought about it, but he was starting to. This was perhaps the hardest thing to deal with, he imagined, in the horse race of normality. The years went by, and sex (at least the images of socially unacceptable behaviour that sometimes came to him in nightmares) didn't figure in his son's life, although it did play a role in his mimicking of social behaviour. The special school he attended full time for years and years certainly had a fundamental regulating influence, too. At times, Felipe elected a 'girlfriend' from among his classmates. All it took was for them to have a visitor over and, sitting on the sofa like an adult, legs crossed, an air of thoughtful importance about him, he would start in his fragmented syntax.

'I got a girlfriend.'

'Oh, a girlfriend?' the visitor would say politely.

'Yep. My girlfriend.'

'So what's her name?'

He would appear to be thinking about the answer, scratching his scraggly Chinese wise man's beard, and would raise an index finger, happy.

'Um … her name's Juliana. We're getting married.' It was as if he'd suddenly uncovered a secret plan. 'Yep! We're getting married!' He'd get excited. 'We're going on a plane! We're going to Germany!'

'Why Germany?'

'On a plane.'

'Yes, I know you're going on a plane. But why Germany?'

'They've got soccer!' It was hard to follow the logic of the sequence. In the short silence that followed, Felipe would flex his arm muscles. 'Look! See! I'm the strongest! I've got muscles!' After another two or three gags, he'd be the one to excuse himself. 'I think I'm going to play on the computer!' and then, as if offering consolation for his absence, he'd say, 'You stay here talking! OK? Stay talking!'

On two similar social occasions, the father felt a pang of his old shame, together with a difficult feeling of exposure. We are dealing with (the father would have said, if he'd thought about it calmly the following day, in front of the computer, already encapsulated in the figure of writer) a metaphysical impossibility: my son isn't a normal child, and each day that I hang on to this normality, even just a shadow of it, as a model and reference, I will be unhappy — much more than he will ever be. For my son, this value system is radically non-existent. I'm the problem, he would have told himself, feeling a sudden desire to light a cigarette, although he'd completely given up smoking more than five years earlier (he'd even pat his pocket for an imaginary packet). Come on (he'd have to say): give up this horse race that has driven your life for once and for all. He didn't like the imperative tense, not even when talking to himself in the mirror: no one gives me orders. Stupid pride, it was a farce. He'd spent his life obeying, trying to conform to something he couldn't even identify.

Once, visiting an old friend, Felipe had gone up to the daughter, whom he had never seen before and who was the same size as him, hugged her, and kissed her on the lips. 'My love, my darling! Her my love!' he'd said, unsure in his grammar, suddenly head over heels in love, with the sweeping gestures of the ham actor and liar, but he didn't know it: it was just a scene from a soap opera. Sexual taboos are strong, sometimes terrible — the girl got a fright, of course, and there were understanding smiles all around (there were a million tiny social factors at play at a moment like this, a brief tension between five people who knew one another, as if civilisation needed a little kick in order to readjust to a new situation, which was not the doing of any one person), and the father immediately pulled Felipe away with a discreet complaint along the lines of, 'Greet her properly, Felipe! That's not nice!' — a quick shock of repressive electricity that the boy immediately felt, subject to three or four contradictory stimuli that he had difficulty taking in. Back at home, he got a sermon that was more didactic than oppressive. 'You don't do that, Felipe. You can't just go around kissing girls.' He raised his arms, begging for peace. 'It's OK. Wrong again. God, girls!' He thumped his forehead theatrically. 'I won't do it again. Damn! I yam what I yam!' He glanced around, looking for a quick escape. 'I think I draw a bit.'

Some time later, he changed tactics: on another occasion, at another friend's house, he sat boldly next to the friend's daughter and hugged her, smiling, this time without kissing her. 'She's my girlfriend!' It was just child's play, but the air was tense. The father kept an eye on his son, who behaved himself, but the girl was perturbed by the strange boy sitting next to her, of course, and it ended up perturbing everyone, as if they were faced with an inscrutable bear that was docile, but you never knew what it was capable of. In truth, he was incapable of any aggressive or violent act — not because he was a good person, an Adam straight out of Eden with the purity of the innocent, thought the father in his eternal desperation to call a spade a spade, but perhaps because evil required a mental sophistication that was beyond him. As if good were mechanical, and evil, elaborate. Would that make Rousseau right? He smiled. No: it was as if good were a social value, inherited from others, while evil seemed to be exclusively our own, which was harder. Only once in many years did his school report an aggressive act by Felipe: he punched a classmate after extensive provocation, which left him depressed (the weight of guilt, which he felt strongly) for two or three days, refusing to return to classes.

The father also remembered his own only aggressive act, at the age of twelve or thirteen. He had punched a classmate who had been teasing him for days on end while queuing for the bus in front of the state high school. He couldn't remember any other occasion, nor what cruel, heavy, or ridiculous thing the boy had said, just the violence of the punch, which had given the boy a bloody mouth. He had fallen down and crawled away, scared, saying, 'You're crazy! I'm going to tell the headmaster!' He never kept his promise — he just avoided him from that point on and stopped taking the same bus. For the future writer, that punch (and the news travelled fast) was a moment of pride and freedom, the pleasure and power of brutality. At several other moments in his adult life he had remembered that initiatory punch, something along the lines of: I've always got that as a last resort, just in case. He had often wondered, staring at someone who irked him — behind a counter, an eager doctor, a bank employee, a literary critic, a receptionist with a rubber stamp telling him there was a document missing, a congressman — what if I were to punch this son of a bitch? He smiled at the idea and drifted off, imagining that many had probably thought exactly the same thing, staring at him. I'm difficult, he thought, as if it were a rare quality. How hard it is to keep a lid on my hot head! That's why you go out of your way to avoid people, he mused. That's why you've always taken refuge in shyness. That's why you drink, he thought, exaggerating with a laugh, opening another beer. Which he knew he'd have to give up one day, just as he'd quit smoking years earlier — I have to outlive my son, he thought, so he'll never be alone. I'm the only one who knows him, he told himself innocently, oblivious to the stupidity of his words.

Love came before sex for me too, he mused, enjoying his lie, searching through memory for some first moment. He had never been precocious in anything. At fifteen, he had decided to spend a month of his summer holidays with his guru, in Antonina. Arriving without notice (the world was still without telephones, which no one missed), he had discovered that everyone was about to leave on a trip the next day. But he could go to Paranaguá, a town about an hour away, and meet Dolores's family, who was moving to Cotinga Island, where his guru had lived in the 1950s in a Japanese-style house he had built himself, and which he was now letting his friends live in. A romantic artist's refuge. 'Why don't you go there with them? They're really nice. And you can spend a few days on the island. It'll be a great experience.' Like a character in a nineteenth-century newspaper serial, he had received a long letter of introduction. 'When you get there, give this to her,' said his guru. Still unsure about what to do, he had ended up accepting the mission. From the description he'd been given, he imagined a mythical Dolores: an Argentinean with the gift of poetry, married to an Uruguayan who had a job at the consulate or something like that, never completely clarified — a charming haze of references. And they had four young children. Now they were moving to the island, she and the children, while her husband would continue working in the city. The simple set of words ('poetry', 'island', 'consulate', and 'foreigners') had already given that family a special aura — an idea that he savoured happily. Letter in hand, heart anxious, he knocked on the door of a crumbling, faded, blue historical building, next to other ruins on the main street of the old port town, and an unshaven, grumpy-looking man answered the door in a torn shirt, with muscles, scars, and tattoos — his immense figure filled the doorway, truculent like one of Dickens's villains, and speaking a Spanish that he understood in fragments. 'Dolores has gone out and will only be back at six. Tomorrow they're moving to the island.'

They? So who was the guy at the door? It was one in the afternoon. He spent a while wandering through the narrow streets of the town; it was the first time he had ever roamed for what seemed like interminable hours through a strange town, paying attention only to façades and people, and feeling a subtle solitude work its way into his soul like armour — a feeling that would return to him many times in his wanderings in life. The brutality of shyness. He had a little money in his pocket, but he was too ashamed to go into a restaurant or bar for something to eat. He preferred to eat a sandwich on the pavement outside the market. Later, he discovered a detective novel with a yellow cover at a newsstand and bought it. He went to the main square, sat on a bench in front of the bandstand, and stayed there, reading until it was almost six — the book was so good that he almost preferred to stay there reading than face Dolores. The image of that man closing the door didn't enthuse him. What was written in that letter? he wondered from time to time, raising his eyes from his book. He was using the envelope, which his guru had left open, as a bookmark, but he refused to read it — a transgression he didn't allow himself.

This time, Dolores herself appeared at the door — she looked just like Yoko Ono. He had imagined someone different. He handed her the envelope, which she opened right there as he stood on the pavement waiting, feeling the bitterness of defeat on his tongue, which he was discreetly clenching between his teeth: maybe he should go back to Curitiba and think of something else to do with his holidays. But Dolores lit up as she read the letter and stepped aside for him to enter without lifting her eyes from the page. She had a soft Oriental smile — but she was an Indian. In a kind voice with a thick accent, she said, 'Come in! So you're a poet?'

That was a special passport. He stammered something — he'd always felt he was a bad poet, but his guru tended to be generous about the tiniest little quality; he could find anyone's silver lining. Going into that incredibly decrepit house (with everything in ruins, doors falling off their hinges, crippled sofas, cobwebby lamps, tattered rugs, books lying around in a suggestive darkness of corridors and other doors and dangling curtains, broken shelves, children flitting about, four gorillas swearing in Spanish sitting at a table playing cards for money under a light from the movies, everyone smoking everywhere) was like Pinocchio's adventure on Pleasure Island. In two minutes they had given him a caipirinha, which he sipped happily, feeling the first whoosh of dizziness. Then, sip after sip, he saw a dreamlike sequence of images, surrounded by gracious people. Someone appeared with a guitar and started singing — he was an important artist in the town, Dolores whispered, and ushered him into the kitchen, where she was preparing something to eat. 'Have a seat,' she said, clearing some plates to be washed, then called out a name and talked to someone (her oldest son, he guessed) about a household chore that hadn't been done, but in a low voice. She started peeling potatoes as she talked, asking him about his life. Such a delicate woman amidst that mess — and he tried to explode all of the prejudice in his head, to be reborn purified in a freer world. He was on a mission.

He took another sip of caipirinha, which bitterly burned his now liberated soul, and suddenly he saw Virginia, the daughter who was almost his age, beautiful as a porcelain doll, with whom he fell instantly in love and foresaw in a split-second a full life all the way until old age, maybe even on Cotinga Island, surrounded by kids, living on the fringe, as if he could make poetry of his life; and he started mentally writing his first legitimate love poem: stars, sky, lips, night, 'love' rhyming with 'dove'. But the flirtatious Virginia seemed more interested in a movie-star sort, a good-looking guy of about thirty, with blond hair and green eyes, his athlete's body always shirtless, a professional diver, another of Dolores's random guests. And he was a good villain, the type you saw in films, the little poet started to discover between the lines. The guy had his eye on the booty in the Argentinean ship *Misiones*, embargoed for bad debts in Paranaguá Bay and tended by its last four sailors (the eternally smoking, card-playing guests), still hoping to have the right to something when the legal imbroglio was sorted out. The treasure chest, the father remembered, was the bronze propeller of the bankrupt ship, to be acquired with a touch of popular fiction: to get it, the axis would have to be sawn off under water, with the propeller previously tied to enormous floats, and removed on a dark night to get past the marine police — and finally sold in another region for a supposed fortune. Every week the sailors would show up with some object stripped from the already ghost ship, left to float in the bay like a dead whale — bunk-beds, fans, pieces of copper. They sold everything they could to survive.

His fifteen-year-old self had savoured that enchanted world, together with his always-full caipirinha, listening to the artists' music and smelling the aroma of cannabis, which he also tried for the first time. He then had to be taken out back to throw up, whereupon he saw a diffuse light shining over the treetops in one of the few moments when he managed to look up. They gave him water, lots of water, and in a flash he was positive that he was dying, that he would never escape this physical hell, ironically at the best moment in his life; it was impossible to cure himself of this feeling of nausea, the invincible dizziness, the world that wouldn't stop spinning, the monster in his head — he would have done anything to be able to sleep, but it was impossible. Everything spun interminably, no matter how hard he squeezed his eyes shut to disappear in the darkness, until, by some miracle, the day dawned. He woke suddenly, drool on his face, his whole body crooked on a two-seater sofa in the dark living room, where a few slivers of light that looked like imponderable blades of dust penetrated. He heard a fragment of a conversation coming from the kitchen ('That kid almost died.' 'No one realised he'd hardly eaten anything.' 'He's a good kid.'), and he closed his eyes again, feeling protected, his head buzzing. But, with the curtain jerked open in fits and starts because the mechanism had got stuck at the top, the sun restored him to life again and, still dizzy, he had a cup of coffee and ate some buttered bread, ready to help with the move. The night before had been their going-away party, explained Dolores. 'Are you feeling better? We were worried about you!' Yes, he was practically new again. 'Nothing like youth,' she said laughing.

Nothing worse, he concluded several times that month as he tried to attract the attention of his aloof muse. But, all told, things were good: even suffering offered a beautiful frame for life.

That afternoon, they left for Cotinga Island in a robust whaler stuffed with suitcases and small items of furniture, a good stock of food, plus a cooker and a gas cylinder, not to mention those unlikely migrants, himself among them by chance. The sky blue, a pleasant breeze playing on his face, he felt an intense, happy melancholy. Sitting atop those floating fragments, the whole world — every detail, the silhouette of the island appearing straight ahead in a whimsy of trees, hills, and rocks, the colour of the sea, the muffled roar of the boat's motor, everything — seemed to have been designed exclusively for him, promising a future of absolute happiness. In less than twenty-four hours he had gone through a brutal initiation-ritual and come out whole, stronger, now part of a brotherhood, almost an adult. All he was missing was love — and he imagined himself entwined with the lovely little Indian who, perched on the prow like a living São Francisco riverboat sculpture, was arguing at the top of her lungs with her older brother, until Dolores calmed them down.

Like his father, Felipe also thought that a woman was a good idea, an innocent infatuation, which he illustrated with the flying hearts he'd learned at school, which began to tame, in a good sense, his drawing, and then his painting. Little by little, the careless splashes of paint in his art classes (still under the impulse of the automatic drawings that replicated his impromptu theatre) gave way to patient, careful brush strokes, which illustrated a pre-naïve world because he had no other references. In his mind, the father imagined, everything was in everything at the same time. Painting was reproducing, and even the distinction between reality and fantasy seemed unclear when verbalised. Just as Felipe wanted to marry Juliana and travel to Germany, he also wanted to be a professional football player, at the centre of an absolute, smiling egocentrism, always with the enthusiasm of one who had just discovered a magical solution when his soccer team was having a bad game. Wearing a black-and-red striped jersey, the club's flag draped in the window, he'd say, 'Look! I go there! I play with them! I've got the jersey! So I go and kick a goal! What do you think? Good idea?' He would wait anxiously and happily for his father to approve his plans to save the team. But his father couldn't approve — all he could do was transform his reproval into affection, with a bear hug, 'How about just being a supporter, like your dad?' He tried to explain to his twenty-five-year-old child why he couldn't run onto the field to play, but it was an absurd task; the words used (professional, athlete, adult, rules, training, hiring) all fell into an esoteric bucket of references that were beyond him, as meaningless as 'last week' or 'the day after tomorrow'. But the weight of social expectations, whose codes he knew, supplanted all other needs, and his son resigned himself, saying, 'Oh, that's OK. No problem. I'm just a supporter then,' and his eyes returned to the TV, where his team was losing another match.

In this male world before and beyond naïveté, the father mused, the image of woman was yet another piece in a world without perspective, attitudes without essence or intention, gestures without the dimension of time and its concomitant responsibility; as if the biological impulse crumbled halfway there, unable to find a social scaffold that gave it meaning and history. In this case, if the father was right, which he wasn't sure about, in his son the idea of 'love' really did find the absolute dimension dreamed of by poets: a brief abyss beyond time and space, transcendental pleasure, and communion with the universe — and, at the same time, the most absolute solitude. Yes, love always came before sex — wherein reality finally seized and took possession of us without remission or frame.

At the all-day painting workshop that Felipe happily attended twice a week, the charm of his spontaneous style found the discipline of forms, basic, attractive colours, and some technical skill. His acrylics were eye-catching and became a household success. Every month he would proudly display his wallet filled with the money from his sales, always accompanied by harebrained plans to get rich and buy the world; or, failing that, to buy another Atlético jersey, which was just as good. For him, buying a car, collectors' stamps, or a jersey was all the same. Everything was pantomime; attitudes that mimicked what he saw and heard, transformed into pure gesture, detached from their original utility. Which was exactly what happened with painting, it seemed — painting was less the realisation of a personal project (which didn't make any sense to an eternal child), and more the fulfilment of a social role, a place you occupied that defined you.

As with any acquired skill, the taming of his style wasn't without some loss, which was the consequence of education. The father, paranoid, often imagined his son was receiving too much help — complete nonsense, he eventually realised. For example, he still didn't have the fine motor control (neurological maturity) in his fingers to draw with his brush the subtle contours between the objects in his paintings (which were basically always colourful drawings, as if he had captured and isolated a frame in a cartoon). The contours were thick, at times impatient, irregular, and smudged, and his patient teacher often did it for him. This bothered the father, obsessed with the idea of absolute 'authorship' — a whole web of cultural references that defined 'subject' and an inalienable individual as an isolated entity in a glass bubble, supposedly his own boss — as inaccessible to the boy as any other abstraction. The father's concern with authorship didn't make the slightest sense to Felipe, for whom painting was a pleasurable activity that he shared with his friends, a socialised game. He was visibly proud of a job well done — stimulated by the sincere enchantment that his paintings provoked. The main thing, the really important thing, which was a great achievement (his dense father began to realise), was that his son's painting went beyond a mere repetition of forms. He already had an unmistakable style that came from his drawings and passed into his painting; he had, within the limits of his syndrome, his own way of looking at the world, and his work expressed it.

Felipe also adopted the stance of an 'artist', someone who defines himself as such of his own accord, which was always potentially petulant. In the adult world, the father knew, calling oneself an 'artist' was almost an act of social insistence, forcing open a door into a libertarian Eden, where one didn't answer to anyone — a shadow of a paradise lost. Felipe liked to tell others that he was an 'artist' (when he was physically looking at one of his paintings, because it was only then that he remembered), which he sometimes did leaning on the wall next to his work, hands in pockets, one leg crossed over the other, the tip of his foot touching the ground, in a pose that he completed by leaning to one side, like a master of ceremonies of himself, an unconscious parody of pretension — of any kind. And he always enjoyed it.

The father envied his son, capable of putting 'artist' on a par with 'astronaut' and 'soccer player', and forgetting them all in the next instant; there was nothing easier, it seemed, than fulfilling a social role. The father had always refused to say, with feigned humility, 'I do a bit of writing' — the alibi of those who excuse themselves, of those who wanted to go to the party but hadn't been invited. This had never been his case; he had always had an aggressive autonomy, bordering on sociopathy. At the same time, for many years he had been ashamed to call himself, outright, a 'writer', and his greatest anguish came from the fact that, for a decade and a half, he had nothing to fill the space in the sentence when people asked what his profession was. To say 'I write' would have been like confessing something absurdly intimate, equivalent to one's sex life or family problems, confessing what one dreams of in the dark, the misshapen matter of desire, sharing one's breath, confessing that pile of useless but arrogant, pretentious words, kites flown on vanity. For all those years he had felt the ridiculous weight of being a writer, someone who published books that got no response, books that no one read, and had bravely resisted (at least in that he was successful) the comfortable consolation, the itch some people have, almost always pathetic, to blame the world for their own choices. It was simply a fact that one had to deal with alone, he imagined, like a boy scout, for years on end, a peasant, revolving in his world which was ten metres in diameter, until he became a lecturer, got a job, one that really seemed justifiable, a job that afforded him a sigh of relief, the perfect alibi. He was, finally, someone, and someone of some importance even. A fine figure standing before the blackboard! That is, he earned some money with the sweat off his own back, as his father had wanted, and as his father's father had done, all the way to the beginning and the end of time.

'But where's the Nietzsche of your adolescence?' the father sometimes asked himself, looking old in the mirror. 'In my childhood,' he answered, smiling, his teeth sharp and crooked. More precisely, he fantasised, on Cotinga Rock, a large rock in front of the house on the island, with a view of the bay, from where one could contemplate on the horizon the lopsided spectre of the *Misiones*, the classic pirate ship he had always wanted to live in, already tilting from the voracity of its last ghosts' little raids in order to survive. I left my childhood on the rock, he repeated, correcting himself, like a verse coming back in bits and pieces. Dolores and the children, himself included ('Your hair's so fine,' she used to say, running her soft hand over his head), would sometimes spend hours gazing at the sea and talking in low voices about everything in life that seemed transcendental, their rapture intermingled with little everyday trifles. When night fell, the postcard-perfect full moon once again lived up to the cliché, spilling across the ocean in a scintillating carpet, which he absorbed with the desire to also be a part of nature, along with Virginia (who, a metre away, was a thousand light-years distant), anticipating a long life full of self-evident meanings that would unfold one after another until they reached some pantheist plenitude (from that time on, the idea of God was absent from his life). *A Charmed Life* might have been the name of the painting, if he'd thought about it — neoclassical figures from childhood books living out an epiphany of authenticity.

It wouldn't take much to get there, he imagined — all that was needed were a few small corrections, softening touches, discreet omissions, and some back-up captions, otherwise, so much reality would be unbearable. Like in Freud's dreams, however, in which absolutely everything was false, except the terror you felt, in a sweat, until you suddenly opened your eyes and collapsed in the safety of the real world, everything was false in memory, too, except the peaceful ecstasy it evoked as it inhabited you. In the library that his guru had left on the island — books swollen with moisture, victims of dripping water, eaten by silverfish, bound to one another by spider webs or elaborate wasps' nests — the little bookworm moved forward with the voracity of an archaeologist, reading one book after another in the total freedom of Dolores's chaos, Plato's republic revisited. Puffing on cigarettes (he learned quickly), he read *Confessions*, by Rousseau, and *In the Mesh*, by Sartre, and for a few moments had the sublime feeling that he knew everything he needed to know in life; only Virginia was unable to see it. In the kitchen — restocked with basic supplies once a week during visits from Pablo, the children's father, a thin, kindly, mysterious figure, with delicate gestures and a quiet voice — the battery-operated radio played Miriam Makeba's 'Pata Pata' a thousand times a day. As he turned the pages of the book he was reading, he translated the song's irresistible chorus into Portuguese as 'there's a flea on your rib, pata pata', still entrenched in the pleasure of childhood.

There were no fleas, but mosquitoes — such that even in the heat he preferred to wear long sleeves, like a Mormon, and tried every possible way to escape them or shoo them off, from blowing a halo of cigarette smoke around, which was useless in the face of those fierce squadrons, to (as a last resort) a bucket of cold water from the well, emptied straight over his head three times in a row, in a purifying bath in the bushes accompanied by cathartic Tarzan roars, which made everyone laugh, except Virginia, indifferently combing her long hair. The nightly caipirinhas helped anaesthetise their bites; and when he ran out of cigarettes, he gathered up the thousand butts scattered through the house, tore them apart, and stored the tobacco in a tin for budget rollies made in a paradisiacal ritual on the rock at sundown. This memory (forty days and forty nights on the island, without returning to the mainland) merged with subsequent ones from his years with the theatre group, until it all came unstuck, each piece of memory in its own destitution, in a tiny diaspora that was to imbue everything with meaning — like Dolores's death due to an overdose a few years later. He returned to Curitiba a small grown-up, bought his first packet of cigarettes, Capri (which were shorter than normal ones), at the bus station, and savoured the smoke with hues of melancholy. On his personal thermometer, he figured, that was one of the happiest moments in his life.

It was a metaphysical measure unfamiliar to his son, who handed him a pen and paper and said, 'Write *bus*.' His son never did learn to read or write, but he was able to copy letters on the computer keyboard and navigate through the interminable sequence of Google pages, with total mastery of the mouse and the apparently self-explanatory logic of Windows and the whole system of saving, reproducing, and transforming files and programs from Word to Photoshop. One of the most technologically sophisticated inventions in the history of the world could be manipulated with great ease by his son with hardly any instruction — something like that was bound to be the runaway success that it was. The boy knew how to create new files (which he named FELIPE, or FELPEI, or FLIPE, or ATLTEICO, or ALTLETCO, always with one or two letters out of place). He knew how to write a few words, only in capital letters — his name, his soccer team, his sister's name. The bus he was looking for was his soccer team's bus, which he'd seen somewhere and now wanted to find on the Internet so he could use it as his desktop wallpaper — substituting the previous one, as he did almost every day, in perpetual renewal: the Brazilian flag, Arena da Baixada Stadium, a photograph of his sister or himself in a suit (unlike his father, who had reluctantly used a tie five or six times in his life, his son loved to wear a suit and tie, and took photos of himself posing like an artist, which he then imported into CorelDRAW and captioned *FELIPE*. He put Atlético's emblem at the top and a few other photos around himself, like an altar, printed it out and put it in a picture frame until a new work came to replace it). His father wrote *B U S* — and he rushed to the keyboard, where he fell into an endless maze of Internet pages, until he returned with his pen and paper.

'That's not it! You didn't get it! Write *Atlético bus*.'

'You're better off going straight to Atlético's site,' his father tried to explain.

'Not there. I didn't find it.'

'Then why don't you paint the Atlético bus yourself?'

His face lit up like that of Dexter, one of his favourite cartoon characters, and he snapped his fingers, raising his eyebrows, acting himself like a character.

'Humm! Good idea!'

In his picture, the bus would have eight wheels in a row, and a smiling face in each window. All of his son's characters were inexhaustibly happy. Even the duelling heroes with clashing swords smiled as they fought, fell, and died, to be reborn smiling in the next picture.

Time passed. The father looked for signs of maturity in his Peter Pan, and they were there, but always as pantomime. At the exhibition organised by his art teacher at a shopping centre, where the whole group spent the day, Felipe didn't want to watch the latest Walt Disney movie, *Over the Hedge*, because it was 'a kiddie movie'. At the same time, he was capable of spending ten hours in a row (unless he was dragged away) at the computer playing Asterix & Obelix, grumbling interminably and getting irritated when he couldn't get to the next level, or watching *The Powerpuff Girls* every night before bed.

Felipe had a hard time accepting new things or changes in his routine, always preferring the familiar, and his father had to make him watch new programs with him all the way to the end until he discovered that the new thing was interesting. In this repetitive universe, soccer slowly started to become a powerful stimulus. Soccer, this nothing that fills the world, mused the father; precisely soccer, an institution almost superior in importance to the UN and which at the same time concentrates in its upper ranks some of the greediest and most corrupt figures in the world; a sport that, no matter where it sets down roots, is synonymous with fraud, transformed into a giant, tentacular industry, creator of myths, the most powerful money-making, time-occupying machine ever invented, the definitive triumph of the masses, the greatest circus of all time, the producer of vast emotions about nothing. The father got irritated every time he thought about it; he, too, was a slave to that defective dance in which there were never more than five passes in a row without a mistake, a sport whose umpireship wasn't even remotely honest, not least because it was impossible for them to see everything that went on (there were grotesque umpiring flaws in games all over the world). Nevertheless, he thought, we gather around it to roar, souls turned inside out — because football, that irresistible nothing, had slowly become for Felipe a reference of possible maturity.

Soccer has all the right qualities, sighed the father, trying to think the opposite to what he really believed to discover something new: above all, the notion of 'personality' that the team represented for Felipe, including the very difficult ability to deal with frustration — defeat. In the first few years of his fascination, defeat meant an instant change of team, rummaging through drawers for a better jersey to wear. Then, little by little, he began to realise (through social mimicry) the secret importance of fidelity, and his view of the game changed. There was also the element of novelty: unlike the FIFA computer game that Felipe played almost without thinking, repeating the same passes thousands of times, a real game was almost always unpredictable, giving a wonderful dimension to the idea of 'future', no longer just something that he already knew and would repeat over and over for the rest of eternity. Perhaps, mused his father, confused, the thousands of people who pack stadiums are seeking precisely this brief enchantment: the simple future, the power to surprise the wind of time in the exact instant in which it transforms into something new — a feeling that everyday life is unable to provide. The millimetric abstraction between now and later at last became a part of his son's life; a football championship was the teleology that he had never found elsewhere.

And the game has other qualities, thought the father, counting them on his fingers: socialisation. The world was divided into team supporters, through which it was possible to clearly classify people. Whenever someone new came over, Felipe would ask what team they supported. 'Fluminense,' the visitor would say. Felipe would head for his jersey collection and come back wearing a Fluminense jersey to hug the visitor. Diplomacy out of the way (he knew the operation was always a success), he would come back into the living room wearing an Atlético jersey, which got laughs out of everyone. There was the concept of championship: games, for Felipe, were no longer random events with no relationship to one another; it was through the notion of a championship that he finally grasped the idea of a calendar. Like in the Bible, the world was divided into parts that succeeded one another until the 'final battle'. The word 'final', incidentally, had a metaphysical weight, which, to be perfect, involved a penalty shootout — for Felipe the crowning moment of football mythology.

But there was one thing that was still tricky: knowing when a game was a part of the Brazilian Championship, the Brazil Cup, the South American Championship, or the state championship. The very notion of states, Paraná, São Paulo, Minas Gerais (he was already able to point to a few on the wall map in his room with some accuracy), the breakdown of Brazil into regions, or the idea of a 'national team', which could have players from a number of different clubs representing a country — all this, in Felipe's innocent mind, was a jumble that he still hadn't fully grasped, although he could now distinguish between the South American and the Brazilian championships, aided by patient, insistent, and recurrent explanations. But it was also a vast, vague world that required reinforcement at the beginning of each new season. There would never be an end to this, the father knew — because soccer also allowed for another mythical dream, that of eternal return.

But there was another point, another little utopia that soccer promised — literacy. It was the only area in which his son had any reading skills. He was able to distinguish most teams by their names, typing them into the computer so he could download each club's anthem in MP3, which he then sang happily, in fits and starts. He still confused similar names (Figueirense and Fluminense, for example), but was able to read most of them. At any rate, they were only random words. Which didn't matter, the father felt. Apart from a brief broadening of perception, learning to read and write would be an abstraction; if it were possible, if his son fully learned to read and write, he speculated, he would be torn from his instantaneous world of present meanings, without any metaphor of passage (he didn't understand metaphors; as if words were the very things they indicated, not the intentions behind them), to inhabit a world rewritten. He will never be a part of my world, thought the father, suddenly feeling the depth of the abyss, the same one every day (and, perhaps, the same one that lay between all parents and children), yet the boy continued to throw his arms around him every morning for the same circular hug.

'There's a game today, son!'

The boy smiled, exultant.

'Today?'

'Yes! Atlético and Fluminense!'

'Then get Christian!'

Christian was a neighbour who was also an Atlético supporter — every time there was a game, their apartment became a grandstand of fanatics.

'Yes, he's coming.'

'Great! We're going to win! Four–nil!' and he showed his splayed hand, looked at his fingers, laughed, and said, 'Oops! I'm wrong! Five–nil!'

'It's going to be a really tough game,' said the father, a pessimistic supporter. 'How about two to one?'

Felipe paused. He held up his hand again, now showing three fingers.

'Three–nil, that's all. What do you say?'

'OK. But it's going to be tough. Are you ready?'

'Yes! I'm strong!' He raised his arm, fist clenched. 'We can do it!'

'Let's see if we win.'

Felipe nodded, and added, arm still raised, his laughter easy, 'They're going to eat our dust!

It was one of the first metaphors of his life, copied from his father, who also laughed. But, so the image wouldn't be too arbitrary, Felipe pretended to eat dust. Black-and-red flag duly unfurled in the window, make-believe warriors, they finally headed for the TV — the game was beginning once again. Neither of them had the slightest idea of how it would end, and that was a good thing.